Claude & Marcel

Janis Spehr

Claude & Marcel

Ours is not a century of paradises
Henri Michaux

my bright star

Claude & Marcel
ISBN 978 1 76109 243 5
Copyright © text Janis Spehr 2022
Cover image: Alexandre Boucher from Pexels
Despite making every effort, the author has been unable to contact the likely
copyright holder of images used in the text

First published 2022 by
GINNINDERRA PRESS
PO Box 3461 Port Adelaide 5015
www.ginninderrapress.com.au

Contents

CAFÉ

joie

March 1937

She is the star of the sea, the unique lover with ever-open arms as she rises from the waves. She dives, dolphin-like, lost to view then breaks the surface closer to that distant line between water and air. She rises, spins, armoured in spray; she is Thetis, she is Ceto, she is Asterah, haloed by the sun, gilded gold and silver in the light.

'Lucy!' I stand anchored to the tideline by low-heeled leather shoes and call her, avoiding the long slow suck of the ocean, the lapping foam. She disappears once more, becomes a trawling figure moving away until she is no larger than an insect hovering above a midday pool while I remain on the shore, the speck of sand, the grit in the oyster, the thing that sticks.

I will not call again. She defies me because she can.

Henri watches beside me, smiling: he has seen it all before. 'You know she always returns.'

But he doesn't know how much she likes to lose herself. She wants to become a wisp of ether or a sliver of light which writes lines on paper, to float free from flesh, aligned with white smoke, or the mist which hovers above early morning waves.

The sun stabs the water; the sea becomes a harsh mirror filling my eyes with salt. Dazzled, blinded, I wipe them clear with the scrap of silk Henri hands me.

'See, here she comes.'

My eyes heave her through the water. I become her spent and frozen body, labouring to land, the blood chilling her veins, her lungs rasping. I choke on ocean, expel it, amphibious no more. With each drawn breath I haul her in until she crawls, vomiting like an infant, up the sand. Membranes of water stream from her as she stumbles, stands, born again in merely human form, teeth clattering, skin shaded blue as lethal air. She tears the towel from my hand, punishes it over her body; shaking, she drops the rough cotton at her feet.

'I went too far.' She expects reprimand, she invites solicitation.

I say nothing. I hand her the glass of champagne.

'Suzanne!' My name refracts to splinters in her mouth shattering the aqua and silver day as she turns her face up to the sun. The wine warms her; this last week she has lived on nothing else.

She stretches like a cat then laughs. By the time she hands Henri her empty glass, her skin has dried. She pulls her pink cotton dress and blue cardigan on over her costume, the new daring two-piece for which she has starved herself. We sit down on the English tartan rug. Seabirds gather expectantly.

She glances with disdain at the food I chose at the market this morning: apples, strawberries, smoked salmon, bread. Only the wine, carried from St Malo on the ferry, bubbles swirling then dying, holds her interest. She sips, grave as a communicant; Henri proffers elegant slivers of fruit on a knife point, which she rejects.

'I will only take them from Suzanne.'

I know better than that: if I offer a crust of baguette or a dark plum, she will laugh and turn away to Henri with a pretty pout. Henri and I smile at each other then give up. We are drugged by the sun and waves, too lazy to do further battle. She lies on her back while we eat, watching a ship slide along the horizon.

'Where's it from?'

Henri takes up his binoculars, studies it for a moment then hands them to me. The flag is a black spider in a sea of blood.

Lucy studies its stereoscopic progress then shudders. 'Going to Spain, to Franco.'

Henri, a calm island rarely disturbed by currents and tides, corrects her, tells her such a vessel would be out in the Channel, out of sight, that this is merely some boring cargo boat headed for Brest. Neverthe-less, we eat in silence for a while; then Henri says that if the spider be-gins to crawl all over Europe, he will leave and work his passage to Asia or South America.

Lucy cuts two pieces of bread and arranges them on a plate. 'Breton says…'

'Oh, Breton.' Henri makes an obliterating gesture.

Out in the bay, the sun glints on the stone fortress built long ago for the English queen.

Lucy rises and runs to the shoreline, gathers detritus from the waves and sand. She collects pale, salt-streaked shells, sea-washed pebbles and fragments of pink and brown seaweed. All these she lays on the bread, to make a sandwich. She places it before us with a flourish. 'My dear friends…'

She cuts it in half, hands one part to me and the other to Henri, who looks at it solemnly.

'This sandwich is too beautiful to eat. The sandwich must not be consumed. It longs to dance and sing.'

Lucy crowns him with the sandwich; she places it solemnly on his head. Henri unfolds himself, glides like a tall bird across the sand and spins slowly, arms outstretched. His bizarre hat becomes a platter for div-ing gulls. A piece of dried pink seaweed falls across his forehead as he sits.

'Bravo! Bravo!' We cheer and clap. We proclaim Henri a clown, a trickster, an acrobat.

We leave the sandwich for the birds and I pack up the picnic food. A track of grey earth flattened by tourist feet winds between the rocks which skirt the beach. We push the bikes uphill until we crest the land and see the strand of silver birch which lines the road.

We turn westward. Henri coasts along with Lucy sitting between the handlebars while I pedal stolidly behind. A motor vehicle trundles by, hooting courteously. We pass a scarecrow in a field of giant cabbages. Further along, golden cows graze and chew. The sun sheens the waves to iridescence and forces sweat down my sides. Lucy sits with her face out-thrust to the breeze like a figurehead on a ship's prow. She rides, balanced as a cat, between Henri's arms, her smile abrading the air.

In Paris she was a pallid-haired ghost haunting the apartment, drifting for hours in a miasma; impenetrable, lost. At night, neither eating nor sleeping, she inhabited childhood, heard the taunts of schoolgirls, 'Jew, traitor Jew,' as Alfred Dreyfus stood trial, charged with passing secrets to the Germans.

Memory wore her sanity thin: it was still winter when I said suggested the island.

'Let us go! But let us take Henri too.'

During the crossing two days ago, she was bilious and wretched but now she swings her legs, a ballerina light as foam. Henri is infected; their laughter mates on the strong Atlantic breeze.

When he reaches St Aubin's village, he disregards the turn the main road takes and flies straight on, pulled back to the sea. We enter a web of backroads narrow as paths. Drystone walls rise on each side. The air is moist, green. Gnats hover in gentle black clouds. We plunge on, turn a corner; the lane finishes in a patch of grass guarded by stone.

'Where now?' Henri asks, the stranger here, looking first at Lucy then at me, our memories scattered with summer days on the beach, first as children then as girls, prisoners in white muslin, longing to be free.

We wheel around, turn another corner, meet another wall.

'We're lost!'

'You know we can't get lost on the island.' I use my sensible voice and lead them back the way we have come.

We reach a junction leading to another dense tracery of paths.

'This way.' Henri points to the right.

'No, this way!'

We glare at each other, thirsty and trapped by these sunken roads. The sea's percussion batters us.

Lucy's disorientated, her gaze shifting back and forth from distant ocean to stone walls. 'Follow Suzanne,' she tells him.

I push off confidently, hear Henri mutter and curse.

'Trust me.'

They follow me left then downhill through a blur of wild cherry and chestnut until the track widens and we burst through to the headland overlooking St Brelade's Bay. Below is Portelet, the tower on the tiny island laid bare by the tide. There's the sweep of coastline and the sheet of blue-green water stretching to France.

We stand outside a tumble of stone, now too wind-worn to tell whether it was once a Norman fortress or a farmhouse. Henri adopts a lordly slouch in an archway as Lucy takes the camera from my basket. He stares straight ahead, unsmiling and inscrutable, the expression he projects in all photographs. She's always trying to catch him off guard, fix him with an emotion, but Henri remains elusive. He belongs to no one: he submits but is not tamed.

'Let's go,' he says, after she presses the shutter.

We follow the bay's curve while the tide turns and covers the beach. This is an island of saints; ten holy men and the Mother of God give their names to its parishes. We ignore the small church named for St Brelade, that Cornish wanderer, and lead Henri to the building beside it, walking past tombstones garlanded with black fungi and marble flowers. As always, I genuflect automatically when we enter, the nuns' training impossible to eradicate. Henri, that proud apostate, refuses to bend his knee.

'This is the Chapel for Sinners, so you see, it's the right place for us.' Lucy leads him to the single window at the end.

Above this clear salt-washed eye, the flat yellow angel trumpets his news with the unfurled scroll. He is beauty beyond sex, his long hair floating behind him, his gown brushing bare feet. The woman before him in the blue mantle turns her face away, as though willing him gone.

This is the only whole story left, the other paintings mere fragments from a dream God once had. Corroded, decaying, they slept beneath a blanket of plaster and outlived the idol-smashing fanatics of the religious wars, were resurrected at the end of our own Great War. They are a popular sight for tourists, those pilgrims of the modern world.

'He's a honeybee sent to fertilise the flower.'

'No, he's reading the riot act, telling her to do as she's told.'

'You think she is too hard, *too rebellious against the male?*'

'Yes, but he will break her down, make her see sense.'

'God doesn't have to be a vicious father.'

'My father was God.'

We have heard about this, the child Henri forced to his knees in front of the dead man on a dead tree, lectured by priests about the body's uncleanness so that at night he lashed himself with branches torn from the garden. There are no beautiful stories for him here; the paintings bring memories of guilt, pain, mutilation.

As we leave, I surreptitiously dip my finger in the font and tell him this place was used last century to store the local militia's guns.

'Very sensible.'

He is much more interested in the Aladdin's cave nearby, with its clots of old saucepans hanging from the roof and clocks which dispute the time. There is a bolt of red and gold striped satin, a set of boy's tin soldiers, some of which are amputees, a jumble of shiny bracelets which will blacken the arms in an hour.

'André would love this,' Lucy remarks, as she always does when she comes here, referring to our friend the eternal scavenger, the haunter of junk shops and bargainer in flea markets.

'Oh, Breton,' says Henri, but this time refrains from the gesture. The lurking blue-chinned hulk who owns the shop is absent today; the thin freckled wife with darting eyes keeps watch.

'Look! Look!'

At the back of the shop stands a headless man wearing a suit. We strip him down to his bald sex then I become a wall, protecting her, watching the transformation with one eye, warding off the curious with the other.

She slides on the stiff white shirt with its detachable collar, pulls on the navy blue trousers, slings the vest around her shoulders then shrugs on the jacket.

I fashion the bow tie into two silk wings, fasten the silver cuff links, drape the heavy silver watch chain intended for a distended bourgeois belly then go seeking a hat. There is one for a boy, sprouting a green and blue feather in its band, which I carry back in triumph. The shoes are too large and make her clop like an arthritic donkey so she abandons them, trips barefoot across the dirty floor. She is Claude Cahun once more, beauty beyond sex, performing a beautiful lie.

The good woman behind the counter draws in her breath and crosses herself against this blasphemy. To placate her, I buy a pair of pale pink satin evening gloves, pieces of Second Empire frippery which reach to the elbow. I catch myself in a mirror, dowdy, competent-looking in my brown skirt and dark green cardigan. Claude comes strutting up behind me offers a deep bow, holds out her hand to me.

I cannot resist, I burst into a wild siren song, 'I want to stay faithful, guard your honour / Seek peace, obey / Fear, serve and honour you / Until death...' courting her, as I did in the twenties, when I was her art deco paramour, Marcel.

Henri who has been watching us slyly, drops a shoulder, tips his head to one side and shambles up to Claude. Grovelling, quavering, he is Plume, the little man so afraid of being kicked that his very behaviour invites it. They circle each other, Claude the little street tough pushing Plume, mocking him until he falls, curled like a fetus.

I pull him gently to his feet. As he rises, Plume disappears, becomes once more our debonair and distinguished friend. We buy the suit and pack Claude away. Everything goes into the basket on my bicycle.

'Let us take tea in the afternoon.' Lucy affects a high-pitched, English schoolmistress voice.

We turn inland. The sound of the sea fades to a monotonous murmur. Always it carries a history of war, conflict, grief. I look west to the Bay of Quen, think about de Rullecourt leading the remainder of his force into battle one day in January 1781. One thousand men drowned trying to reach the island. It is said that later that night, shawled women walked on the sand, harvesting the pockets of the dead.

The new owner of the Café Gitane speaks French with a harsh Breton inflection. She has a face carved from weathered rock, a lean body and black hair held back by a dull yellow band.

'Oh, where is Jean-Pierre?' Lucy asks.

'He left,' the woman replies, and says no more. She serves Henri and me vanilla-flavoured pancakes dusted with icing sugar.

There is no tea on the menu so we drink cider with sour golden foam, comment on the stylish new bentwood chairs. The flyblown oval mirror in its gold-painted frame still hangs above the fireplace with sepia photographs of bearded fishermen and their boats.

Lucy eats nothing, drinks only a glass of water then goes outside. While we finish our refreshments, Henri tells me the name of the new proprietoress, Madame Madec, and says that the dark-haired girl stacking plates expertly on her arm and carrying them to the kitchen is her daughter, Gabriella. Madame Madec, Adèle, is a widow but, because they are very recent arrivals, nothing else is known about them.

'Well, that will surely change. It's hard to keep secrets in this place.'

After that, we fall silent. We are the dotted line which forms the triangle, our history cratered with ambivalence and mistrust. There is part of her which wants him all to herself, has always wanted that since they met in 1925 and she made his double-gazing portrait. Months it took, coaching and wheedling and flirting, before he would sit before her but she had her answer in the image, those two faces rearing serenely toward the viewer. Michaux will always keep a space for himself. He will never be her homeland. And yet, still, sometimes, I resent the hours they spend together, deep in poetry and art.

Now, he places his cutlery neatly together. 'Perhaps we could return in summer for the flower festival, throw tulips and roses at each other, or collaborate in making a beautiful float for the parade.' He laughs and pushes away his plate.

'Perhaps.' I let the word hover inscrutably as a Buddha in a pagoda. 'There won't be any more festivals, if there is a war.' I remove his cutlery from his plate and stack it beneath mine, replace the knives and forks as the waitress swoops.

Michaux watches, smiling ironically. 'Oh, Suzanne, always organising something.'

I make no reply. He sees her genius, her games, her mad teasing and sorcery. He only glimpses her habits of self-destruction. He knows nothing of her ether-hot spirals to oblivion, the night I called her back when her heart that *mysterious misfiring motor* faltered and stalled. He knows nothing and his ignorance is my power so I finish my cider and sit, tension locking my limbs, until her shout summons us.

As we emerge, the descending sun strikes my eyes. I open them to see her wearing only the swimsuit, hanging from the trellis at the front of the café, her flesh burned golden, the sand striated by shadows from the latticed wood. She's raided the satin gloves from the bicycle basket and these hang on her like sloppy pink forearms. One foot has its shoe, the other is bare.

'Get the camera!'

She has left it sitting carelessly on the top of the basket for all to see. Onlookers sitting out the front of the café regard us curiously but smile. We are entertainment on a spring afternoon.

'No, not there. There! Yes, that's right!'

I become a dummy, a mere ventriloquist's doll, her slave. I move forward until the image fills the tiny pane in the camera. The shadows leap towards me; their strange grid snares me. I'm a prisoner of light and dark. I press the shutter. The mirror flies up. The light writes its miracle. I turn the spool which winds on the next frame.

'Again! Again!'

I click the shutter, wind the film, click the shutter.

'You! Hey, you! Get down from there!' Madame Madec carries a broom in her hands. Her hair flies out like a malignant halo as she advances towards us; she looks so absurdly like a witch that we all laugh.

'Get down from there! I don't want you damaging my property!'

Lucy drops and runs, hides behind me, then Henri, then escapes around a corner of the building, chuckling like a naughty child. The witch lowers her broom and returns inside. I watch her through the window, giving directions to the girl loaded with dirty plates. Lucy comes creeping back, motions me towards the trellis as she hoists herself up.

'Get down! If you don't get down I'll call the police!' This time, the witch approaches holding a garden hose. She flays Lucy's face and breasts with a sprouting jet of water, whips it around her naked legs.

Sopping, dripping, Lucy cringes on the sand. Our towels are still damp so we use the English tartan rug to dry her. The woman, victorious, once more vanishes inside. The people at the tables applaud. We take a bow, supremely amused.

By the time we reach the hotel, the first stars preen themselves and the air lifts the scent of herbs from the garden behind. We are securing the bicycles to the railing outside when a frizzy-haired woman, her cheeks wearing a harried menopausal flush, crosses the courtyard.

'Why, it's Sylvia Beach!' I open my mouth to call out but Lucy grabs my arm and steers me away.

'Let her go.'

'Sylvia has a friend who lives in Trinity,' Henri murmurs.

'Perhaps, if we're lucky, we will see the waddling earth mother as well.' Lucy laughs.

But it is not Adrienne Monnier, the plump grey dove, who emerges from a car parked across the street. This woman is tall and lean, dressed in a dark suit, very American-looking.

'They're worthy ladies.' Henri is referring to Sylvia and Adrienne, his friends, and who can argue? After the big crash in '29, Sylvia didn't pack up and go home like so many of her countrymen; she stayed and soldiered on, held to French soil by stubbornness and her love for Adrienne. For years, their bookshops have faced each other on the rue d'Odéon, English-language and French, twinned magnets for writers, students, thinkers and people who just want a warm fire on a cold day.

'Sylvia has had a very difficult time financially in recent years.'

'She does look rather worried.' I watch Sylvia greet the other woman affectionately.

'Ah, well,' Henri continues, he who is always ready with the juciest gossip, 'Adrienne has a new love now, a young German photographer. Sylvia has been pushed out of the nest.'

'Who would have thought the fat woman capable of attracting someone else! Is the German so very ugly?' Lucy laughs again.

Henri looks at her calmly for a moment then gives me a glance of sympathy. I don't know whether to be grateful or to slap him, so I gaze indifferently back. I know more than he does: Lucy will never admit how hurt she was by Adrienne's refusal of her book, years ago. It put an end to our friendship, to our evenings spent in their company and the visits to the shops, although I still have a photo of Sylvia taken by Lucy in 1919, before things went bad.

The car disappears up the rise. The air chills suddenly. A thin moon rises from the waves. We turn towards the hotel, its windows gleaming yellow like the eyes of a friendly beast.

But I think about Sylvia throughout the evening, while we change in our room then descend to the dining room to eat mussels with a salad and drink Muscadet. I imagine her pain and confusion, how it would feel to be cast to one side for someone else. I would feel that my life was ended. I would want it to end.

Lucy eats a few mussels. When I coax her to clear her plate, she turns down her fork, leaving a minor shipwreck of shells. Henri eats the remainder of the seafood then announces he will take a stroll.

'You will call by to say goodnight,' Lucy calls after him.

He has a room on the ground floor. His smiles enigmatically but does not reply.

We have the large, front-facing room we are always given, the one with dusky blue walls and a brass bed covered with a rose-patterned quilt. The staff here think nothing about our sharing this room. We have always posed as sisters, two decent middle-class spinsters who had their sweethearts killed in the war, women who live a retired life on money from a provident family. Over the years, we have become famil-iar and are not thought about much.

None of them know that we are joined by passion, not blood, our own vows to each other taken and consummated long before we stood side by side at the wedding of her father and my mother, a civil wedding because no church wanted any part in joining a Jewish man and Catholic woman. Later, the four of us attempted festivity at a well-known restaurant but its mirrors and brocade couldn't disguise the taste of horsemeat. Outside, all news was of the Battle of Verdun: the rumour that our troops were shooting their officers in cold blood hung like poison vapour in the air. On the way back to our apartment, we walked arm in arm, steps crippled by fashionable sheath-like skirts.

Now, we put on coats and sit out on the balcony. Another guest is playing a gramophone; a tinny thread of Richard Tauber rises towards us. The red eye of a buoy winks steadily.

'Tomorrow I will take the film to be processed at the chemist.'

'When you have made the prints, perhaps you can give one to the café owner.'

We laugh then are silent. In the background, the sea murmurs its lullaby. I think of the empty house I saw near the churchyard today, the one with diamond-paned windows and a garden for the cats. I open my mouth but before I can form the words she turns to me.

'That house near the churchyard… There is enough room for a studio.'

'We could grow vegetables…'

'We could have a whole farm!'

'No, it would smell too much.'

We sit thoughtfully in the darkness. The ocean is flat, glassy; its frail track of silver is broken when the moon goes under a cloud.

'We could be safe here, when the war comes.' (Suddenly, we are no longer saying *if*.)

'You're only safe when you're dead.'

I take up her hand, stroke the white wrist with its highway of veins and pale ridges of scar tissue. She turns, kisses me. 'We should stay.'

'Yes, but if we do, there must be no more transvestism.'

JUDITH

courage

October 1940

We wake in the morning to find that black spiders have crawled all over the village. Through the bedroom window, a grey sky issues icy drizzle. The ocean is a fleeting dream behind mist.

We do not learn of the desecrations until we descend the stairs where Madame Rondel is ladling batter into a pan. Lucy wrinkles her nose; she always maintains that our housekeeper stinks of butter, that a congealed creamy substance oozes from her pores, but I can only detect a whiff of flour and laundry bleach when I stand next to her at the stove.

It's Madame Rondel who mentions, casually, after giving us triumphant details about her success at finding cheese at the shops, that the Germans have randomly daubed their national symbol on houses across the island. 'It happened to the Moulins and the Blanchets and the Taylors.' Madame's small eyes dart sideways while she pours coffee, then she places the plate of pancakes in the centre of the table.

We eat slowly, digesting her news in a silence which is punctuated by the distant thunder we barely notice now. Outside, thin autumn sun has beaten back the mist and rain to clear a space for the plants; the cactus near the front gate stretches up spiny arms. Mignonette frisks, warming her nine-year-old limbs as she spars with a drifting leaf.

Madame Rondel reaches into one of the cupboards, investigating our ever-diminishing supplies. She has small dainty hands and feet, must once have been a slim girl, before child-bearing and cleaning people's homes thickened her. 'There seems no reason why their houses were chosen, they are all fine people…'

'No, there wouldn't be.' I cut her off sharply, then, seeing her offended intake of breath, collect the plates and join her briefly at the sink, a gesture of conciliation which only makes matters worse as she sees it as a reflection on her competency. The house is large and it would be highly inconvenient if Madame Rondel were to take her services elsewhere. I do not want to clean, or cook, even though I'm quite capable of whisking eggs and roasting meat. Lucy is utterly useless, would rather starve than put a pot on the stove.

When her father married my mother, two streams of money merged: into this wide and steady river we regularly dip a modest earthenware jar. This extraction buys us Madame Rondel with her blackcurrant eyes and knuckle-swollen hands, her lingering half-note of laundry bleach.

Now, we stand together in uneasy solidarity, our eyes drawn down to the corner of the building visible from the window. We watch the officers in their grey uniforms moving around the grounds of the hotel, which is a designated recreation centre, a place where they recuperate from the stress of their purifying mission. Local women cook and clean there too, as well as providing other essential services. We see the garden; like ours it is one of the few on the island not turned over entirely to produce. I gaze with almost voyeuristic pleasure, my eye rakes clots of pink roses and the brave trumpets of yellow lilies until Lucy pushes away a plate littered with crumbs from a half-eaten bread roll. Madame Rondel turns and momentarily frowns, shocked by this waste at a time when the population barely has enough flour. She sees me looking, smoothes out her scandalised expression, picks up the plate and puts it down in the sink, then sets off to forage for us, basket over her arm.

We bathe and dress then harness Mignonette and Tiger. (Omelette, who died eleven days before the war began, has given his flesh and bones to a clump of robustly sprouting daisies.) Tiger is a grey tabby, ferocious in name only. Mignonette, patched black, white and gold, delights in bullying him, boxes his ears; Tiger hisses at her pathetically, completely subject to this gleeful domatrix.

'Tiger, you have the heart of a lily.' Lucy picks him up and we ease our way past the cactus, which must have grown from a cutting no larger than a child's thumb but now looms so close to the edge of the path that unwary callers occasionally lose blood. Lucy won't hear of its removal to a more benign location, refers to the plant as 'my spiky angel'.

Despite the sun, she has wrapped herself in a turquoise cashmere shawl, as though it might conjure a sparkling summer ocean, not the flat pewter sheet before us. However, if you were to look closely, you would see that the shawl has been mended with tiny patches of vivid cotton, red, cobalt and purple, and that the fine, camel-coloured wool trousers I wear are darned, almost invisibly, just below the hip. Most of our pre-war clothes show this battle against disintegration but we hold on to them, these garments we love, as though they are talismans. The alternative is to buy the cheap rayon which composes most of the meagre stock displayed in shop windows in St Helier.

'Come, let us walk.'

We proceed along the path, arm in arm. The sun, a sallow disc, is too near the centre of the sky this early in the day but that is because the Germans have moved it

**In order to conform with Central European Time,
all watches and clocks must be advanced one hour...**

When we first read the orders posted by the conquerors all over the island the day after they landed, we laughed at the correct German English marred by the wrong preposition; didn't laugh as we continued reading the circumscriptions they intended to impose upon us.

We close the gate and walk the path which borders the cemetery. Mignonette races ahead, pulling at her lead, taunting a recalcitrant Tiger, who follows, meowing piteously. Old tombstones skew like teeth in an elderly maw but there are several granite rectangles, very erect, grey and new, bearing German names.

From a point overlooking the beach on which no civilian is now allowed, we watch a gang of men labour with concrete, working for the King of Prussia. Who would have thought that old expression, coined after the war of 1870, when France groaned beneath the burden of reparation payments, would find such a new and interesting life this century? At a distance, the men are stick figures; as we draw closer, they remain that way. Emaciated, with only thin clothing against the approaching winter, they lift and carry the grey blocks which form the walls designed to repel Allied troops and tanks. All over the island, these ramparts are being constructed by slaves then reinforced with guns which thrust seaward. Fragments of polyglot sound drift from the beach as we stand gazing down: it sounds as though they are building the Tower of Babel.

The desire to distinguish language drives Lucy forward, disregarding my pleas, beyond the sign which warns that pedestrian access is forbidden and down the disused path leading to the beach. As we move closer to the slaves and their overlord, my ears distinguish something impenetrably Slavic as well as the musical open vowels of Spanish. We know that many of the men are Russians captured by the German armies and put to work for them.

We reach a small viewing platform made years ago for tourists and look down to black rocks at the edge of silver-grey sand. The ascending sun has begun to warm the air and it might be one of the last days suitable for swimming but this is no longer possible because the Germans have planted the ocean with death. (Several of the soldiers lying in the cemetery are victims of their own mines.) Sentries patrol the beach where Lucy and I once swam, porpoise-free, where we caught crabs in rock pools and sifted the sand for shells. Now, worry about those we love submerges regret about this curtailment.

Jersey is a place for exiles, of Bonnie Prince Charlie and Victor Hugo and the displaced utopians of 1848. Some of them must have gazed southward, as we do now, towards our country, partitioned between the conquerors and the ageing *generalissimo* with his motto of *Patrie, Travaille, Familie*. Where is André, veteran from the last war? What has happened to Jacqueline and little Aube who once bathed with us here?

Where is Lucy's dear Desnos, in particular peril from the Aryans? At least Michaux is safely away, a piece of European flotsam swirled by Asian tides, although the rumours which reach us, patchy and intermittent as radio broadcasts on a night of heavy cloud, say that he is now in the Vichy zone. We know nothing of our brothers but when I venture a comment to her about Georges, who is still in Paris, she merely smiles.

'Georges will always take care of himself.'

We link arms, stare out at the sea. The time we spent living in Paris, *on the street where everything happens, where everything goes by, where nothing knows you* runs behind my eyes like excerpts from a silent film. A swift flock of evil birds drones briefly overhead then disappears, on its way to England.

'Well, where are Roland and his Olifant when you need them?'

Invoking the medieval *chevalier* and his magic horn makes us laugh but if the sound had a colour, it would match the leaden waves which froth at the feet of the group below. One young man barely out of his teens stumbles under his load, sucked down by the wet sand. The fore- man, whose look of lean health tells of his privileged status with his masters, shouts at him in Spanish. I understand the tone, if not the words: perhaps contempt sounds the same in any language. Then the overseer hits the young man across the face so hard he almost falls. A rosary of blood splatters the sand.

Lucy cries out, as though the blow was for her, and the overseer glances abruptly towards us. He speaks to the boy then leaves the group. As he approaches, he yells at us in English but we pretend incompre- hension.

'Let him climb. If we are to be shot, then let us make it an effort for him.'

He hears me, scowls then chastises us in rough ungrammatical French, using the familiar *tu*. His hair is as black as the young Spanish boy's but his skin is Celtic-pale.

On impulse, I respond in English. 'I'm sorry, neither my friend nor myself read German.'

'You know very well what the sign says.'

I can't place his accent. Beside me, Mignonette hisses, a patchwork virago wanting to be gone. For the first time in my life, I wish I had a dog. I feel Lucy's anger simmering like a witches' brew. In vain, I will her to silence.

'You are a bully and a pig! You will have no men left if you treat them like that!'

He smiles. 'Plenty where he came from. The boy is godless scum, the son of Republicans who fled to your country after they lost the war. I killed many like him. If you have a sheep with a disease, you kill it so it doesn't infect the whole flock.'

Suddenly I understand his proficiency in Spanish. 'You fought in Spain, for the Nationalists.'

'Yes, I fought against the Reds, the men who killed priests and raped nuns.'

We digest his comment in silence. His eyes are clear grey, deeply set, lit within by the slow-burning fuse of a fanatic. It's impossible to see what he sees, or tell how he sees us. All I know is that I must deflect him, protect us.

'It is true that there were atrocities on both sides but Spain isn't in this war.' My response sounds feeble; conciliatory.

He smiles again. 'Hitler thought Franco wanted too much. He always drove a hard bargain, General Franco.'

'But you work for Hitler against England?'

'English mercenaries killed one of my uncles and a cousin in 1921. The English had their boot on our necks for hundreds of years. I'm no great lover of the English.'

There is nothing we can say to that. We make our apologies and retreat.

We climb back to the footpath, where a young German soldier, not an officer, accompanied by one of the local girls, has not noticed our exchange. He smiles at the cats but frowns when he sees what I'm wearing. Perhaps, in his comparatively short life, this is the first time he has seen a woman in trousers. Does he think I am some sort of dangerous pervert, just because of the way I am dressed? I feel suddenly vulnerable, pincered by hostility. I almost hustle Lucy along, dragging Mignonette on her lead so that she yowls at my cruelty. The girl, who is potato-faced and slightly overweight, with lank pale brown hair, someone who has never had the local young men pay her any attention, ignores us and gazes adoringly at her prize.

I take Lucy's arm as we pass behind the hotel, its back windows blank, shutters closed. My thumb lies against her wrist; I can't tell whether the pulse I feel is mine or hers. In the nearby streets, people go about their business as instructed.

Banks and shops will be open as before.

On her cheeks, raised red blotches bubble and swirl. As the sun finally vanquishes the clouds, she bursts out, 'England took me in, gave me sanctuary!'

'I know, I know.'

It is a primal story. I first heard it not long after the afternoon in 1909, when we first stood, stiff as two staring dolls in pantaloons and petticoats, in my mother's drawing room. Behind her, Maurice smiled then gestured as though presenting a gift.

'This is my daughter who has just returned from boarding school, across the Channel.'

Her long blonde hair still hung childishly below her shoulders. She looked at the green brocade wallpaper and sniffed. Mamam extended her hand, choreographing welcome. I was haughty, impersonating a young *mademoiselle*, my hair bundled and clamped to my head with ivory-tipped steel pins as I glowered at the blonde girl.

'These look painful as a crown of thorns.' she said some weeks later, and the hair came tumbling down, covering my breasts, winding with her own as we became *a sphere in movement – a rolling geometric shape with no edges, no top or bottom.*

We had taken down the crucifix above the bed but the mirror

showed its absence, the shape inscribed against the dusty wallpaper of the smallest bedroom, never used. We drank from a jar of water sneaked from the kitchen, cooling our mouths smeared with each other, and binding each other with stories.

While I trickled my fingers along her thighs, she told me about the mad mother she never saw and about the convent school during the years Dreyfus and his supporters clamoured for justice, the school she had to leave due to the antics of one of her darling little classmates, a baby-faced girl with plaits.

That sweet little girl, with big doe eyes, the one who was always first to volunteer for blackboard cleaning and flower arranging in the classroom spat in Lucy's face. 'Jew! Filthy Jew! You don't belong here! Go away!'

When the charming little girl was later questioned about her behaviour, she denied all responsibility and said that her friends had made her do it. 'They said that they wouldn't play with me if I didn't punish the Jew for what her people had done.'

The little girl, who looked as though butter wouldn't melt in her mouth, who looked as though she was made to sing lullabies to kittycats, her long plaits tied with white ribbons, was given a severe reprimand by the Mother Superior, instructed to say several Hail Marys and apologise. By that time, Lucy had stopped eating, was screaming in her sleep and refusing to leave her room. Her father was summoned. He listened to his daughter and decided she would be safer in a foreign country.

I steer her gently down the street behind the hotel where we once spent summer holidays. 'History is relative, and we are all formed by our own.'

'I know, I know.' But her gaze withdraws from mine. She will not give up her Arcadian idyll; and in England there was Jane, her first love, the general's daughter, now married.

As we pass the hotel, we see the spider which has started it all, scrawled blackly within a circle. We do not pause, only glance at it obliquely; nevertheless, the image sears me like a brand. Someone has had courage. He turned the conquerors' national symbol to a sticky daub on the wall of the hotel. He was not to know that they would retaliate, use it against innocent people.

Lucy urges me on and we pass sedately, gazing straight ahead. It doesn't do to show too much interest in anything and we have already shown quite enough for one morning. We take the cats home beneath a sky shredded by the sound of approaching aircraft.

The house smells pleasantly astringent of lemon polish; Madame has set wood in the fireplace and supplies for our lunch. I prepare a salad and pour wine. Through the diamond-paned windows, we watch gulls and petrels wheel above an ocean patterned by clouds but all through the meal we feel the spider crawling, scrabbling and disgusting, covering everything with slime. It's almost three months to the day that the invaders disembarked, barely wetting their polished boots as the sun glazed the water ultramarine, and the shells rained down on St Helier and St Peter Port. The men in the grey uniforms were orderly, even polite, but knew better than to trust us.

Next day, notices appeared.

We will respect the population in Jersey; but should anyone attempt to cause the least trouble, serious measures will be taken.

I mention this to Lucy as I collect the plates then cut up a precious orange, carefully cleave the last passionfruit taken from our vine and serve them with a meagre slice of goat's cheese laid on a dark leaf. We eat with ceremony, using small, Victorian, bone-handled knives, a wedding gift to my mother from a distant cousin on the occasion of her marriage to Maurice.

'So…you think they will take "serious measures"?'

'It seems they already have. They were not going to let a challenge to their authority pass. It might give people all kinds of ideas.'

'Ideas are one thing, action quite another,' I say as I peel a segment of orange. Beneath its withered skin, the fruit is surprisingly sweet.

'Well, the second without the first is not possible.'

'There are spontaneous actions, surely?'

'Yes – but a fine line between those and mindless violence, often.'

We bat these ideas quietly about before domestic matters intervene. Madame Rondel has forgotten to provide us with soap. (The fact that she has forgotten to provide us with any item indicates her level of anxiety about the current situation.) I search at the back of the cupboard beneath the sink, retrieve a dried twist which fails to lather. All the time, the aircraft pass overhead, lower than usual, cold beneath the sun, the roar of them entering our bones.

Lucy hums part of an old pre-war show tune and gazes distractedly towards the ocean.

I hand her the square of linen kept for drying but she throws it aside, like a petulant nine-year-old. As usual, she seeks to abnegate what small domestic responsibilities our housekeeper leaves us. I normally indulge these tantrums but the events of the day have worn my patience down. My hand fumbles underwater; I clink one of the china cups too hard against its saucer. When I hold it to the light, a hairline fracture runs from lip to base.

'Don't expect me to always be Martha to your Mary.'

'Who are these women?' She asks this innocently, as though she has not read the New Testament from cover to cover. 'I don't know them.'

'Liar! I' pick up the cloth and whip it across her face, hard enough to sting.

We glare at each other like cats then she stalks offstage. I glimpse her as I stand at the sink, watch her wander in the garden, see her snap off flowers and collect shreds of shells and flat dry pebbles procured originally from the beach. She takes her cargo and distributes it like so much floral garbage, leftovers from the annual Festival of Flowers (although that event was not held this year). I watch her at this anti-horticulture as I sluice grey water over crockery.

Madame Rondel has left us a wild hare, snared by her husband, in a marinade of red wine and tiny onions. (The recipe also requires bacon but there is none.) I set it to simmer in an earthenware casserole dish on the stove as my flame of anger subsides.

I know that last night Lucy slept with the radio, heard her rise and leave our bed early in the morning as the cold breeze harried the final leaves from the birch outside our window and lifted the lace curtain screening the sickle moon. I heard her moving around as she twisted the dials of our oracle. These night prowls are becoming more frequent and there are bluish shadows beneath her eyes. Now that Henri is gone, there is no one here who shares our life. If she breaks down, who do I turn to?

I am drying the injured cup when suddenly she looms behind me, wearing a large square of dark transparent cloth which she has pulled over her head and fastened at the neck with a noose of string. I let out a small exclamation, drop the linen towel. At a distance, she is a blind zombie, a bulbous parcel of flesh but as I move closer I see the ghost of her face through the fine mesh. What is the meaning of this self-imposed purdah?

I am quoting André Breton as I tug at the bow of string: *there is always a corner of the veil that expressly demands never to be lifted.* Perversely, I take the veil away and we twirl, two strands whirling; drawn into enchantment, we kiss, reconciled.

'Let us go and look at what these vandals have done.'

'That's a good idea — and anyway, we need to buy soap.'

This time, we walk north, away from the sea, up the gentle swell of land leading to the village. We note that the Germans have left the bourgeoisie alone: the doctor's house, and the substantial stone dwelling which is the holiday home of a British industrialist, are clean. It is only the humble cottages which have been besmirched. We walk past these quickly, barely glancing at the gleaming black obscenities but as we turn a corner, see an elderly couple surveying the desecration. The assailant has applied the paint with Expressionistic vigour (even though he would surely say he despised modern art). Sticky black tears have rolled down the wall and pooled in the yard where three chickens scratch. There are geraniums at one window and a slate tile missing from the roof. This mean shack, their frail carapace against the elements, has been branded by the juggernaut but left standing so that its inhabitants will be daily witness to this violation.

We stand there, silently. The man holds his wife's hand. I feel their shame, mirrored on Lucy's face.

She waves, timidly. They look back, not moving. We all watch each other now.

Wordlessly, we progress to the village's main thoroughfare, drop down the two steps to the cool sanctuary of the grocers. We buy the soap, gritty and unscented, think longingly of the slender perfumed bars which, until a few months ago, came from Paris but the victors keep the best things for themselves – food, wine, soap, shoes – while the natives are forced to wear clogs and wash with grease. Goods reach us intermittently from the 'Free Zone' in the south but they are made mainly from carrots, their quality abominable.

As we step up to the footpath, a villager dressed in dark fisherman's trousers and guernsey glances skyward, gives a guttural exclamation, an echo of the stuttering engine above. We look up, see a falling star, a comet which becomes a scarlet splash at the horizon. We feel the hiss and spit of the fiery kiss as the plane hits the sea, see the flaming doll trapped inside.

Lucy cries out as though scalded, leans against me, shaking. People stare, their eyes jerked from the sky but they say nothing, look away again.

I steer her on until we reach the Café Gitane, pass beneath the trellis where in another age she gave joyful commands as she hung like an acrobat.

The wind has sharpened. She collapses into a chair outside. Through the window, Adèle Madec smiles as she swings around her kingdom, setting down plates of pork cutlets, sausage and eggs, the kind of food which must remind her new customers of Bamberg and Ingolstadt. A man sitting near a group of officers looks out as I sit kneading Lucy's hands, shivering, although my face is dry and my feet steady.

He is scarcely a man, this Baron, although not an aristocrat either, the name an ironic reference to his hybrid heritage, Norman gentry suffused with a nineteenth-century English injection of railway and textile money. Now he unfolds himself with an etiolated graciousness properly enhanced by Saville Row. The wind lifts a lock of his light brown hair as he takes Lucy's arm and ushers us inside. Madame Madec approaches, frowns at us although she is properly deferential to our escort, almost bows. He opens his mouth but I cut him off.

'My sister isn't feeling well.'

'Oh, yes, your…*sister*.' Adèle Madec gives the word a sardonic inflection, as though she is a voyeur at the window of our history. I stare at her coldly, disputing her power to strip us bare.

'Please, the lady is distressed.' The baron gestures with an expression which on a less exalted person would be beseeching.

Courteously, the officers vacate their table. Adèle Madec disappears into the kitchen and returns with a glass of water so full that when she places it carelessly on the table it slops over. Lucy blots the spillage with a napkin then drinks. Her breathing evens, her gaze focuses. I thank our rescuer, embarrassed by my earlier brusqueness: in these times, distrust contaminates even basic civility.

'The least I could do.' He resumes his seat, crackling the newspaper, which barricades him from the surrounding carnivores.

Madame Madec speaks their language thickly but fluently, jokes with them as she puts down more cutlets and half a brick of butter. Local gossip says that she recently dismissed one of her staff because he was not sufficiently polite towards the Germans.

We watch them, obliquely: they read papers from Berlin as well as the one that they now publish on the island. There is a smattering of the lower ranks, talkative but well-behaved and intent on their food. The only other non-Germans lunching belong to the Baron's class because they are the only ones who can afford Adèle's prices.

It is better not to be seen observing. It is better not to look. It is better to gaze quietly into the large mirror which stills hangs above the fireplace and watch Adèle Madec watching us, waiting for our departure. I plant my feet, ox-like, enjoying her impatience, lingering purposefully until Lucy finishes the glass. I nod and smile to our knight as we leave.

On the way home, we walk along *le route de la baie*, past the hotel, to look again at what started it all. Someone risked death, crept out at night to shame the Aryans with their symbol but now the symbol has disappeared, whitewashed from existence. The wall is a blameless backdrop for the lean uniformed figure which passes before it, on his way to the garden where he will read in the sun or chat with his fellow officers. I imagine the obliterated image breathing beneath layers of paint, something the officers will attempt to dismiss with jokes or perhaps not mention at all; then I think of the tattooed landscape, the squalid revenge of the conquerors against the powerless.

A wave of nausea passes through me; me, the strong one who never gets sick. The sea assumes a malevolent sheen, a sudden purplish-black swell.

I blot perspiration from my forehead and take Lucy's arm. 'Must the weak always lose?'

'Almost inevitably. The human race is divided into sheep and wolves. The wolves eat the sheep.'

'Are the Germans wolves, then?' I'm irritated by her simplistic dichotomy, this neat division, like something found in a biblical story for children.

'No, of course not.' She bends to discreetly adjust a drooping stocking. 'Please remember that my father's father was a rabbi in Frankfurt. Wolves are not peculiar to one nation. Every country has them. The Germans have fallen under an evil spell and this has allowed their wolves to emerge.'

'No spell,' I say, further irritated. Now she sounds like a fairy tale, a modern-day poetaster rewriting Little Red Riding Hood. No wonder the Communists disdained André and the rest of us, thought that we were incapable of analysis and historical rigour.

I adopt a dour materialistic tone. 'The Germans had two economic depressions, not just one. Desperate people turn to extreme solutions.'

'"Spells", solutions": same thing.' She shrugs dismissively.

Somehow, all our words are unsatisfactory, an echo of the botched experiments of the thirties, the doomed attempts to synthesise politics and art.

We continue in silence until we arrive home, open the gate and greet the cats. Lucy's handiwork is still there; as I bend to pick up Tiger. the rabble of wilting petals transforms. I see the word she has crafted, the call to valour, the lion-word which springs from spirit and flesh.

I think about the word as I prepare the evening meal. The wild hare tastes strong and gamey and I swirl the bloody juices with bread, thankful for Monsieur Rondel's skill as a hunter. We eat our fill and collect the glasses and plates.

This time, she picks up the linen cloth without prompting and dries silently, eyes downcast, contrite as a novice nun, using a grace more erotic than any décolletage to arouse me. She leads me to the small room at the back of the house containing a bed with permanently rumpled sheets. There is a careful cluster of photographs: one of Lucy's young smiling parents (taken before her mother was taken away to the asylum); another of her brother; her grandmother, the rabbi's widow who cared for her as a child. An ivory-backed hairbrush, complete with twining blonde strands, sits next to a collection of scent bottles. This is a stage, a set piece to spare the blushes of Madame Rondel. We let her believe that this is where Lucy sleeps but it is a place for passion, not repose. This is our sanctuary from the constraints of public display, a primal lair lit by candles.

'My heart,' she whispers, kissing my neck, shoulders, breasts. 'My other self. Come to me.'

Later, I write the floral word languidly along her thigh then reach across her to the shelves beside the bed for the radio, draped with a decorous frilled cotton cover. (We decided that it is best to hide forbidden items conspicuously, although I did dissuade Lucy from keeping her camera in the bread bin.)

**It is forbidden to listen to any wireless transmitting station,
except German and German-controlled stations.**

At night, with drawn curtains, we attend our radio like acolytes around a high priestess. We venerate her as she transmits the voices from across the Channel, the voices which inform us about the progress of the battle in the skies. Sometimes the nuances of the language escape us but the unctuous English voice is so soothing, it makes the war seem barely believable, a child's game where a chubby fist plops toys into a basin of water. It's a voice so utterly righteous that it is impossible not to hope. We need this optimism, after the lies of Daladier, the fantasy of the Maginot Line, the shame of French cowardice.

'If the English win, perhaps everything will be over soon.'

Lucy switches off the radio and rearranges its gingham cover. 'No chance. The Führer has set his sights on the Soviet Union.'

I smooth the sheets, plump pillows; the room looks used but not dishevelled. We collect our strewn clothes, wrap ourselves in shawls and migrate to the bed canopied in shabby red brocade in the large room at the front of the house. Ancient rugs cover the dark wooden floor. The oval mirror, brought from the Paris apartment, gives back our faces and naked arms, blurred and yellowish.

'Roland and Olifant will not rescue us this time.' I blow out the flame of the candle I've carried to light the way.

'No. It is time to take "serious measures" of our own.'

For a second, the moon finds a crack in the black-out curtain, shows her profile: resolute and melancholy.

'We cannot go riding in, armed with lances, on towering white chargers. We must be stealthy.'

'*Montrer patte blanche.*'* I reach for her hand.

'*Montrer patte blanche.*' Excitement, contagious as fever, suddenly lights her face. 'Let us be chameleons, dazzling acrobats, guerillas who strike then are gone!'

* Literally 'to show a white paw', similar to the English expression 'wolf in sheep's clothing'.

In the darkness of our room, sealed from searchlights and ordinances, rebellion seems possible.

'Some people would call this madness…'

'Madness or…courage.'

January 1941

'Let us blitzkrieg tonight!' She flourishes the scissors and the blades cleave the winter light. She takes a sheet of scarlet paper and folds it. Three subtle creases make a bird's head and body; two more give it wings. She makes another which is turquoise, then one of viridian; citrine; violet. These are our courier pigeons, the bearers of messages, faultless origami branded with words of subversion.

I sit at the Underwood typewriter, scroll in sheets of the lustrous paper bought on the quai Voltaire in 1936 then watch the clacking progress of the metal head as it pecks out its slogans signed by *Der Soldat ohne Namen*. We are bundled into layers, strata of garments which do battle against the cold. She wears a woollen scarf, indigo, which she says is the colour of heroes.

We are the heroes. We are the soldiers with no names.

Clack, clack, clack: *Our revolution is not just for one but for all.* I hand her another scarlet sheet, the red of courage.

She places it flat upon the table. 'I am bored with these birds.'

I imitate a nursery school teacher, adopt a voice for babies. 'Clack, clack, clack, let's make a tidy stack.'

We giggle a little, pause from our labours to watch the snow falling over the group of men gathered in the cemetery, just beyond the window of our fortress.

There are the gleaming cylinders of their cars and the blunt snubs of guns. The men stand in formation, rigid, flanking the coffin, surrounded by generations of granite headstones and a grey wall. The scene is a stone poem, a moment frozen in time, then a sliver of air disturbs the flag, its black, white and red billows infinitesimally and the scene becomes a silent film as the man in the black and white robe reads from the book. The soldiers wait, their uniforms charcoal against the snow while one of them lifts an instrument to his lips, but there is no sound, only snow falling among headstones and being trampled underfoot when they leave. One officer brushes it briskly from his shoulders then climbs into a waiting car which has been posted with sentinels through-out the ceremony.

For the Germans worry about their cars now. Brightly coloured birds fly through the freezing air, brilliant as parrots, bringing dispatches from some warm place far from war and there is no telling where they will land. Once, a whole flock of yellow birds settled on the seat of the *Hauptsturmführer*'s Mercedes. Birds nest in empty cigarette packets which are often scavenged by military and islanders alike. Birds roost on windscreens, gaudy starbursts of blue, purple and orange or alight on benches and seats in streets and parks. All are songs of sabotage. All are gifts from the soldier with no name.

We watch until only markers of stone and the curtain of shrouding white remain. Beyond, the sea is a whey-coloured pall, or a mirage.

Lucy makes six cats, threads them on a cotton string and suspends them in a window, then we pull coats and hats and move silently among the stones.

We stand looking at the upturned soil, the covering for this fresh offering to Thor. His name was Konrad, and he was twenty-five years old. We make up stories for Konrad, for stories are a way of remember-ing even those who we do not know. Konrad becomes a baker's son, then a child raised by a woman of the streets; he is a rogue, now a mummy's boy. He is a student of theology or a street brawler; a farmer or a man who takes the streetcar to an office every day.

'A person can be either a thug or a saint.' Lucy places a purple bird on the freshly heaped mound. 'But they are usually something else en-tirely.'

The bird, this twist of flimsy paper is soon sodden, just a blot of decay but there is no jest, no mockery in its placing. It is a prayer, or perhaps a war decoration which we award the young sleeper who some may believe is in Paradise or in Valhalla. We do not believe that he is anywhere other than the graveyard in St Brelade, caressed by snow and sleet. We walk towards our house, heads bowed. The snow fills our footprints, erases our presence: white amnesia.

We sit in the house with no name and plot. We do not kill, we do not maim (although we have a gun, an unloaded theatre prop Lucy stole during her brief career as an actress). We are the soldiers of the mind.

But always there is danger, not just from our foes but from the friendly villagers as well. Only yesterday we saw Adèle Madec, her lips rouged crimson, flirting with an officer outside the grocer's, a macabre spectacle, as Lucy remarked, like a shark trying to straddle a skyscraper. Her daughter Gabriella, eyes sooty with ineptly applied mascara, stood nearby, glaring at her mother, jealous at being sidelined.

'We must be stealthy as cats,' I tell Lucy. 'Brazen but careful.'

'Light-footed and fearless through the snow.' Her eyes gleam.

By nightfall, the snow has hardened to ice overseen by a thin El Greco moon. We sit in the kitchen, wrapped in rugs, eating cold fried rabbit, the past tense of the struggling furry gift Monsieur Rondel carried in his hands the day before. We drink coffee made from a weed and clean our teeth with cuttlefish. Candles surround us, their lanks of white flame inadequate for both light and warmth. The cats swish against our legs, begging for food. We throw the rabbit bones onto the floor then doze, clasped together on the sofa.

There is barely enough wood to heap the fire and when we wake at two a.m. it is only a smoulder in the hearth. We shake ourselves and stretch cramped limbs.

'Come, it is time for our performance.'

We put on camouflage, for me a skirt of midnight blue and woollen stockings, shoes which will not slip; she wears a fisherman's jersey and trousers rolled up at the ankles, stout boots with hobnails bought from a local boy, years ago, when we were holidaying here with our parents. (For some time, she wrote him poems which he did not read.)

Carefully we fold the typed rectangles of paper, slide them into pockets; then we each clutch up a nestful of birds. We pull on hats, disguise our heavy hanks of dark and blonde, then Lucy announces that she will set off on her own.

'We agreed that we would stay together,' I hear myself plead. I hate this, hate this delight she has in solidifying trust, only to cut it away beneath my feet. I plant them, look at her, try to anchor this latest flight with tensile words. (Why am I always the rectangle, symmetrical and straight-edged, she the spiralling aviatrix?) 'It's too dangerous to go alone. Remember the lessons of the thirties, solidarity...'

'Broken promises and false hopes, always broken promises and false hopes!' Abruptly she bends and vomits, leaves a greyish pool crusted with pieces of half-digested meat.

I turn away in disgust; she fetches bucket and mop. She seems quite calm as she swirls the glutinous muck into the pail of water, as though the purging has emptied her of fear but I see the colt-tremble in her legs, glimpse her eyes and know I must let her fly.

'All right. We will diverge, just for this night.'

**All inhabitants must be indoors by 11 p.m.
and must not leave their homes before 5 a.m.**

As we open the door and cross the threshold, our breath makes tiny bridal stains upon the air. We pause. Briefly, our hands touch. We wait for the sound of German bombers on their way to England but all is silence.

There is a bleak Gethsemane feeling abroad. The darkness is a heavy cloak fastened by a splinter moon. Clouds hide the stars. We know the time of the German patrols but there is always a chance that we will meet a posse of drunks AWOL from barracks or a solitary spy. It is easy to feel caught in a net of eyes. It is easy for the mind to conjure wraiths and fantasies, mirages in a frozen desert.

We glide quietly as ghosts. My shoulder brushes an icy rasp of leaves.

We walk away from the hotel, along the wall which bounds the grave-yard. I know Lucy has taken the pocket camera which folds flat and silent as an illicit love letter. Why does she carry this forbidden object through the night? It is a special piece of insanity, a taunt to fate from which I cannot dissuade her.

'Here,' she says, when we reach the corner. 'Let us meet back here when the moon has moved seven centimetres across the sky.'

I watch her disappear as she walks due north. Did Judith tremble when she went to slay Holofernes? *A woman is on the move. Toward the camp of the conqueror...* Soon she will turn in the direction of the bunkers which are the German field command. She means to hack off their head or drive a sword through their beating heart. Then she will turn into a wisp of air or a ripple of water and disappear.

I tell myself not to become hysterical as I make my way east to the maws carved by slaves from the earth where it rises to a plateau. These tunnels are dragons' lairs, stockpiles of fire-spitting weapons, now guarded by armoured men; I have to find the chinks in the dragons' armour.

I look for the two sentries, see them, bored and twitching the red eyes of cigarettes, make my way in the direction of the primitive equipment, the spades, pickaxes and wheelbarrows contained in a shed nearby. When the guards move off, I drop the packages of leaflets, know that the workers will find them in four hours, when they are driven to work. The Underwood is versatile, multilingual, a Babel-machine; it can type in German, English and French; I would wish for Spanish, Polish and Russian as well.

I also scatter a handful of red folded birds, flecks of blood on the white ground, then retreat, walking quickly. I have no desire to be seized. Here, houses face the sea but no line of light reveals itself through curtains or shutters. I move soundlessly east; hear the batter of the waves before I see the stone wall which curves against them.

I weight packages with stones or chunks of cast-off concrete, thinking that most of the cultural monuments constructed in the West have been built by slaves. The great cathedrals, Versailles, cities such as St Petersburg: starving men dug out the earth with their bare hands or fell from scaffolding, human sacrifices to church and state.

A snapshot of memory returns suddenly: Walter Benjamin, the German friend of Adrienne Monnier's, sitting poised over chess in the Café Mephisto on the Boulevard Saint-Germain, in 1935. A woman sits opposite sits, obviously a fellow émigré; the camera bag at her feet proclaims her a working photographer.

'There is no document of civilisation which is not at the same time a document of barbarism,' pontificates Benjamin, moving his knight against her bishop.

His opponent frowns, runs her hand through her springy black hair then checkmates him deftly.

Such scenes return now with a sepia tinge, elegiac…

I cast down the last packet on the wall. That's enough.

The moon has moved five centimetres across the sky. I turn back towards the bay as a drift of cloud clears. The Great Bear and Andromeda are visible above. I glimpse two silhouettes, locked profiles shielded by a grove of silver birch. I see the uniforms, grey-green and familiar, the hair of one soldier glassy yellow beneath the moon then the clouds slide back; the lovers disappear.

I hold the whole scene, etched like a negative in my mind, the white ground, the silver trees, the black sky, with that blaze of aberrant yellow hair. I file it away, shake my head, summon my wits. Later, I will look at it again but for the moment I must keep moving, focus on reunion. Any lapse in concentration might deliver me into the dragon's metallic claws.

I walk quickly, a trotting ghost, drop down below the track I took to reach the tunnels then begin to cross the grass verge which demarcates the fortifications from the streets. It is then that I hear the car, see the dark moth which approaches the spear of its headlights as it glides down the hill.

There she is. Another moment and she will be impaled.

I step out calmly. I show myself then I am run, run, running as they clamber out, shouting and directing the beam of a torch. I dodge and weave, trying to avoid this strobe as I lead them inland, back towards the tunnels but slightly west where a shallow gully cuts the rise. I'm hampered by my skirt and wish that I had worn trousers. I'm worried that I will slip. There's no mercy in the world.

I plunge on, descending, certain that the sound of my heart will tell them where I am, jump the tree trunk which I know lies across a shallow declension, hear one of them misstep, trip, curse and drop the torch. I turn up the side of the gully and plunge into a thicket of beech.

I can go no further. There's a cramp in my side, as though someone has poked my flesh with a red-hot brand. I wait, propped against a tree and try to control my gasping. How did I get to be so old, so like a soggy tyre on an automobile or a horse on its way to the knacker's yard? I wait, ready to flinch from a probe of light but the darkness is my friend and stays with me.

Silence.

Silence.

A disturbed bleat of notes from a nearby bird.

Silence.

I emerge from the trees; stumble a little because I can no longer feel my toes. In the distance, there's the sound of a car again, becoming fainter. I slide suddenly, catch at a young shoot which bends beneath my grasp, and almost fall. In the aftermath of the chase, I am hollowed out, brittle as an ice-glazed frond of bracken, but I keep going because the moon has travelled nine centimetres across the sky since we first set out. I look for Lucy, thinking she must have fled but there she is, waiting where we agreed. She must have hidden – or turned into a ripple of water or wisp of air.

'My dear wife, you are exhausted.' She takes my hand.

This simple statement moves me to tears which freeze on my cheeks as we make our way towards home, across this world turned to tundra. Once inside, we clutch each other clumsily, waiting for our lips to thaw.

I note that one of hers exudes a thin dribble of blood where it has been chewed, something which sometimes happens when she is tense or frightened.

'Thank you.'

I light a fire in our bedroom but there's not enough wood left to warm it properly, so we huddle together under the duvet, wishing for hot chocolate, but this is just a beautiful dream, like champagne or pretty clothes; like safety. Lucy kisses my breast and tells me she changed her plan and went to the camp where the slaves are housed. She describes pallet beds on concrete, men in rags, their limbs pocked with sores.

'We must take them food, perhaps even medicine, sheets…' Her imagination is a stretched silver thing edged with black bubbles which burst under pressure.

'We have to think about ourselves first,' I tell her quietly. 'We can help no one if we starve ourselves.'

'No, no, we mustn't think like that!' And she is off, full of plans and schemes.

I hold her, make no effort to curb this stream, remember the reasons we left Paris: the white nights of ether madness, the self-starving, the moods of jubilation followed by a despair which left her prostate for days.

Eventually she pauses and I try to turn her mind, tell her about my soldier-lovers, but it only excites her further. She mounts and rides me, my slippery Valkyrie, shouting her climax then turns me onto my stomach and enters me with her hand. I moan and work against her thrusts, bearing down like a woman straining to give birth. My orgasm releases me from the hours of stealth and subterfuge, the hoods and masks placed upon our existence. I turn, gaze into her face as I enter her, my thumb pushing roughly against her clitoris and watch her come again, this time a gasp, a ripple, a dying surrender.

Afterward, she sleeps, fair hair tousled like a child's. The sheets smell like spilt champagne. I drowse beside her, propped against a rise of pillows. The single lamp makes a dark yellow pool of light. The curtains, of charcoal-coloured wool, so dull looking when seen from the street are embroidered and appliquéd on the inside with the moons and stars and planets: red Mars, flesh-coloured Venus.

Passion has warmed the bed but when I extend my foot beyond the duvet I feel the bite of air, see the nail which is already turning black. Earthbound, I will never fly or dissolve to a shimmer. My body is gravid, solid and enduring, a sturdy useful vessel.

I think back to a time before the war, see Claude Cahun draped in golden velvet and pearls which reach her waist, positioned shrine-like in a stone niche. She would be Buddha, a holy man to whom sublimation comes easily or a stone idol impervious to storm or time.

I gilded her face, creased and folded the golden robe so that it revealed her calves and arched white feet, graceful as leaping porpoises. I framed her in the viewfinder, an enigmatic impersonator. I pressed the shutter, captured her flat, godlike gaze, suggested that she angle her face away from the sun.

It was then that I saw the shadow which fell across the foreground. I stepped sideways, carefully erased that phantom.

Click. I moved forward and bundled her hair beneath a metallic mesh cap.

Click. From her pagoda, she joined her thumbs and index fingers to form the vulva.

Click. Her gaze was a locked casket to which I held the key.

Click. Click. I extracted the finished film. Now it was my job to carry it to red-haired Madame Signoret, the St Helier pharmacist. I pushed through buffeting squalls, on into the palm-fringed town.

Two day later, I retrieved the finished prints. There she was, finished, perfect, my own ordained, gold-robed deity, gazing at me from a photo the size of my palm.

I am the hand which brings her to life. I am the straight-edged rectangle which holds the wild image.

Beside me, she stirs in sleep; then I sleep too, our faces touching, porous with dreams.

Ich glaube, die Wellen verschlängen
Am Ende Schiffer und Kahn,
Und das hat mit seinem Brüllen
Der Adolf Hitler getan.
Heine (Oberst?)

la bannière

September 1943

The waves hurl up oyster-coloured spindrift then curl in a gritty kiss to the sand. Spray ricochets from sullen humps of boulders crouched at the ocean's edge.

She walks ahead, impervious to the wind, stretches out her arms toward the cliffs, defying the eddy that would sweep her over. She wears a grey skirt, an ivory blouse; she is swaddled in a grey woollen cape and a white scarf clasped with silver. Crystals star her ears. The wind turns back a foam of lace at her wrists.

There's no line where sea touches sky: the landscape before us is a leaden page upon which drifts of kelp write sinister calligraphy. This script, so much more elegant than our own poor effort, our pathetic promises on an unfurled roll of calico strung hastily across a road sign, rolls and turns, a floating inscrutable alphabet.

We argued about words this morning as we sat poised with pot and brush.

'I want our meaning to be clear: "Our revolution is the true revolution, the way to freedom."'

She pantomimed an obscene gesture, then muttered, head down like a *cochon* seen on the streets of Paris. 'Revolution, revolution. We are merely revolutionary masturbators. "Freedom." "Revolution." These are words now used to sell fruit in the Garden of Eden.'

'Eve ate her way to freedom.'

'Most people don't see that as freedom, they see it as sin.'

I shrugged. 'Freedom. Sin. Who can tell the difference, sometimes?'

I looked at her, at the dull string hair and the reptilian skin around her fingernails. Last night I heard her as she moved around the house, restless, turning on the radio (now forbidden) feeding on the scraps which now pass for food.

She laughed. We debated painting a banner which reads, *Let us show you the way to sin*, but thought that it would perhaps lead the authorities to the island brothels and we have no wish to disturb the women there. Eventually, we decided on our message then chose the time and destination for its placement.

We have left it there, the pale cotton sheet daubed with red, then walked on far enough to make ourselves innocent. Now we stand surveying the colonised territory. To our right at La Corbière, tiers of concrete rise, a military lookout with a searchlight which dwarfs the benign rays from the nearby lighthouse. To our left, sea-facing guns dominate Noirmont Point, their open mouths ready to spit death.

Stone and steel: these are the things against which we pit our feeble bodies.

For there is no lull in the war: the pile of carcasses rises ever higher. We know that in Leningrad snow covers corpses whittled to skeletons by starvation, that men are bones bleached by the sirocco on North African sand. A new French word has recently entered our vocabulary: Drancy, a place where humans are yarded like cattle.

We will break under the weight of this knowledge and beneath the burden of our secrets: the radio; the camera; the gun; her father's outlawed linage.

Our friends are distant, mute; we live like islands, washed by tides of fear and privation which daily erode the banks of stoicism we construct. There is the constant threat of capture, although we have our lifeline, or rather, our death-line, the tablets we always carry with us.

We will break under this weight; but I must not.

It's cold. We descend towards our treasured house, its grey stone walls fortress and sanctuary. The large, woven-cane basket I carry over my other arm bumps emptily against my hip. Across the street, soldiers have cut down some tall elms in front of the hotel, making a clear line of sight to our door. We pass through, feeling exposed; members of a threatened species.

Here is the fireplace, the lustre of old wooden chairs, a brocade sofa taken from my mother's house in Paris. (My brother protested, wanted it for himself but I prevailed.) Chana Orloff's ceramic skull rests next to a vase of lilies. Lucy's collages, those succulent nightmares, hang on the wall, together with my framed drawings of the beautiful, naked dancer made in 1910. (Can it be that long ago that Lucy and I first saw Nadja perform?)

We walk to the bottom of the back garden, stand gazing back at the upsweep of lawn and tumbling clefts of pink and yellow flowers. The small white flower which has just opened is a mirror to the single star which gleams above. Trees cast shadows deep as water across the low stone wall where the cats sometimes play.

She takes my arm. The tide has retreated; the waves show as dark, silver-edged ripples. Soon the moon will rise and spread its patina, turn the ocean to a moving skin of light.

What is the point of saying, 'I love you'? I only wish to be able to think it very forcefully, near you, in the silence.

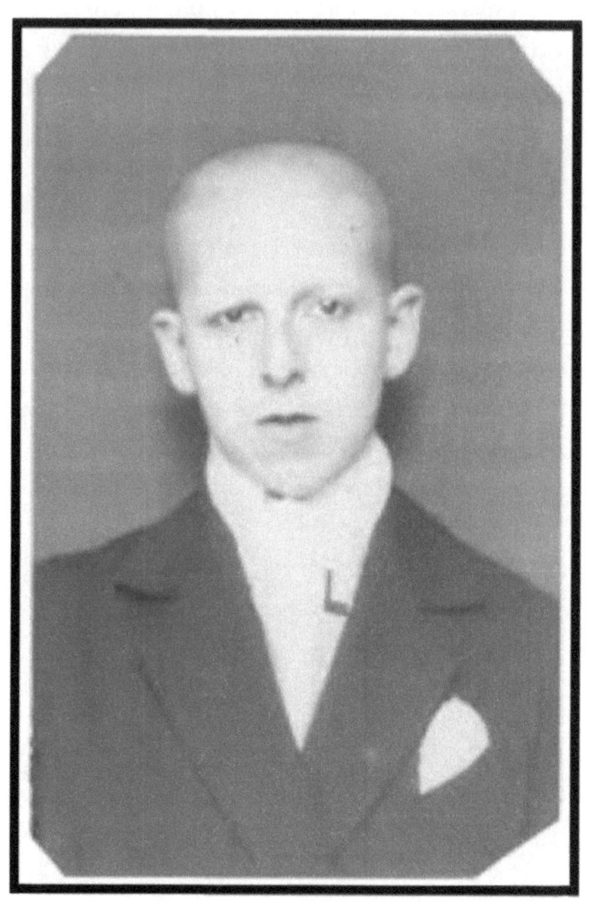

masque

July 1944

The mirror gives back our other selves; we prepare for another performance.

The room is cool, closed to the morning sun. Through the window, I watch her wander with purpose in the garden, clipping summer roses until her hands are full. She wears a three-piece navy blue suit. (It is pre-war but this does not confer a slur on our status; it merely means we are victims of the current austerity.) A snowy ascot wraps her throat, matching her shirt and handkerchief. Her hair gleams in the light, a field of close-shorn stubble.

A thorn pricks her. She sucks her thumb, a wounded prince in an inverted fairy tale.

Seated before the looking glass, I arrange my own disguise. My body is laced into the erotic containment of bone overlain with a slide of white satin. I stand and drape over my head the floral frock with white lace at the collar, cautiously twisting my head one way then the other. Then I pull on the wig, a long dark brown thing, trailing Ophelia tresses. I tame these, wind them firmly and clamp them.

Now for my mask: on goes foundation, paler than my own skin, a feather of rouge for the cheeks and a dark pencil on the brows. Everything must be subtle, understated because I am playing a worthy Catholic matron, someone I should have been and might have been, had not the rose gatherer intervened.

When my visage is finished, I fasten my mother's pearls around my neck as my spouse enters the room with roses which she proffers, gracious as a courtier, but when I reach out, she takes them from my grasp and methodically tears off the petals until they are strewn across the floor like a cascade of blood. Laughing, she offers the stalks, bites my neck hard enough to leave red indentations in the skin.

'You're naughty, my darling.' Carefully, I sponge over these little tracks of lust, continue perfecting my subterfuge.

There is a large, quite hideous hat, bedecked with a type of white organza flower you will never find in a garden.

'Overdone,' opines my spouse behind me, but certain things must be overdone in order to create the illusion of the pious Madame Lemoine.

The rose-pink lipstick must be rather inexpertly applied, to suggest that this is a woman not used to display, a provincial who busies herself with charity and hosts the occasional dinner for her husband's colleagues and their wives. She is someone who performs her weekly conjugal duties in the dark.

I turn away from the mirror to face her critical gaze.

'You look like a perfect bourgeois.'

'Why, thank you, monsieur.'

And now it is time to memorialise us as a couple.

From their place in the polished glass-fronted cabinet, which holds her mother's crystal and silver, the sepia images of Maurice and Marcel Schwob watch us set up the camera with cable release. Marcel, her uncle the poet, laughs from Oscar Wilde's knee. Maurice's face is sombre: how he hated me, only grudgingly allowed me into his home after his daughter refused to eat, her protest at our separation. He thought he would win but our bond was stronger.

We stand in front of a Japanese lacquered screen, beside which my husband has placed a potted fern. He sits on the chair, holding the hand which I place upon his shoulder as I stand behind him. We hold the pose, faces immobile as our postures, in this parody of nineteenth-century marriage. I depress the metal plunger on the cable's end.

'Come, wife, we must away.'

We almost forget to collect the invitation, printed on heavy cream paper with matching envelope, idly filched during one of our nocturnal soirees and requesting the company of Doctor Lemoine and his wife at the St Brelade's Bay Hotel for an afternoon of 'culture and entertainment'. Lucy takes it from the occasional table in the hallway (we are certain that during the night the occasional table turns into a unicorn or a griffin) and we walk into our back garden for a dress rehearsal.

Tiger greets us, winding himself sinuously around my ankles in a twist of cream and grey fur.

'Where is Mignonette?'

We spend several fruitless minutes searching for our calico. The air is limpid, completely still; at least there is no danger of my husband having to chase his hat across the lawn. If that happened, our heads would be right in the lion's jaws.

But it's thrilling: we are taking this great chance all because we learned from the worthy Madame Rondel, now employed at the hotel, that there is a large portrait of the glorious German leader at the head of the main staircase. We desire to honour this in the appropriate way. Each of us carries a paper sash. My husband's is slid into an inside jacket pocket, next to the cloth which bind his breasts and reads, *First prize winner in the fascist beauty pageant.* Mine is folded decorously into my handbag: *Here is the leader against justice and truth.* We debated some desecration to the famous face but dismissed this as an idea for kindergarten children. We do not resort to such banal strategies.

Across the garden, I watch a spindly little man practise his walk, a restrained strut of barely concealed self-importance. It's perfect, the right balance between the swagger of a street tough cherishing an enormous set of balls and a fairy's mincing swish. Privation has starved off much of his fat and he has padded out his belly with rags to form a paunch. From underneath the low-pulled hat, his features are indistinct. He will pass in a crowd of strangers and people we nod to on the street once a week.

He approaches and proffers his arm. 'I have mastered myself. Let us promenade, my dear.'

I take his arm, suspend my handbag over a gloved wrist while he closes the gate at the bottom of the garden. We stroll through a Monet landscape of warm air with sea haze rimming the horizon. Ribbons of cloud drift across a pale blue sky; on the water, the sun slices their reflection into glimmering flickers of light. The trees lining the path throw down stipples of brightness, dapples of shade. All that is missing is a woman in a long white dress carrying a parasol.

I mention this to my spouse, who chuckles drily and indicates my hat. 'Are you sure you're not her descendant?'

We laugh together companionably. I pat his arm and incline my head graciously to a man and woman, unknown to me, obviously bound for the same destination.

'Such a beautiful day,' I twitter to the woman who has on an even larger floral abomination than my own. 'God has surely blessed us with the weather…'

'Don't overdo it,' the little man beside me mutters and steers me determinedly away. Today, he is the practical one with his feet, encased in fine leather brogues, planted firmly on the ground.

In the distance, we see the Baron and several other important landowners who once would have driven expensive English cars or perhaps been chauffeured: now, necessity makes pedestrians of us all. I know better than to greet them; we are mere bourgeois and must wait to be acknowledged – or not. We both breathe out as the Baron's glance slides over us but then we forget him because there is the entrance, the tall painted gate today twined with white flowers. A uniformed flunkey takes the invitation I produce.

'I'm afraid my husband has laryngitis. So embarrassing, don't you think, a doctor being ill?' My frilly laugh again, designed to deflect questions.

The lackey smiles magnanimously and we cross the wide lawn which slopes gently to the cliff edge overlooking the sea. At the top of this verdant rise, trestle tables, draped in spotless white, bear a feast. This is where all the good things have gone: delicious chicken held by wafers of bread, golden pastry tartlets filled with mushrooms, meat and herbs.

There are all kinds of delicacies, even caviar, which we sample, the salty black specks melting on my tongue, making me forget for a moment our meagre diet of starch.

But I am careful not to gorge. It would not be ladylike to vomit up this excellent repast. More young men move around carrying trays laden with glasses of champagne and there is a large beaten silver bowl containing some kind of alcoholic punch. Some of the men drink beer; members of the Field Police pass through the knots of chatter and gossip in their grey uniforms, ominous as shadows. We had been expecting no less than a string trio wearing starched shirts and bow ties but instead see a band which plays German oompah-pah music with heavy emphasis on the tuba.

Hiding our disappointment at the lack of Beethoven and Schubert, my husband and I circulate, dipping and gliding, two dragonflies skimming the water then shimmering in air. From now on, as our conversational circumstances dictate, we are chameleons: for people from Quen, we come from Trinity; for inhabitants of Grouville, we are residents of St John. We improvise, our identities shift from one group to another, we walk the high wire of concealment and deceit. The sea glitters while we sparkle and play.

Well, actually, everyone of us is acting a charade: no one speaks about the war on this warm and hazy day. No one mentions the mountains of frozen corpses outside Leningrad, the horses with their bellies cut open. No one remarks upon the swarm of soldiers now advancing with purpose towards Paris, led by men who fell with silk placentas from the sky. This silent knowledge swirls and eddies around us while we enquire about someone's fine heifer calves or express interest in the fertilising powers of seaweed. No one speaks about carnage on Norman beaches or the blood which stained the water not far from here.

My husband reaches around lazily to acquire another glass of champagne. I shake my head slightly in wifely reproach. *You cannot allow wine to impair your judgement.* He ignores me, hoarsely thanks the bearer of the tray, who I recognise suddenly, with his moon-licked aberrant hair. This young man – I cannot think of him as the 'enemy' – his life is doubly jeopardised; surrounded by a conquered people, yet killed if his compatriots find him out. I watch him, with his back so straight, his boots so shiny and his yellow Aryan hair: what a fine example of the master race he is. He lingers for a little on the edge of our group of chatterers. No smile betrays him but I read his eyes which are trying to read us. He dips his tray; his hips sway ever so slightly as he turns – he's flirting with my husband!

This split-second pantomime goes unnoticed. Fractured light glitters when sun strikes glass. I attend to the conversation in which I am currently immersed, a fascinating discussion concerning the availability of turnips. As my husband slides away, joining another cluster of prattlers, I suddenly realise that, on the edge of the crowd, I have my own admirer.

He is about my own age, this man, mature, handsome (although he will very soon have to start watching the amount of *kuchen* he takes off the table) with dark hair and blue-grey eyes. His uniform tells me he is someone of importance. He smiles slightly and gives a slight bow.

I peep demurely from beneath the organza roses, wondering if he can be of use to me. Well, anything is more interesting than turnips and anyway, from the corner of one demure eye, I glimpse Adèle, emerging from the kitchens at the rear of the hotel. What's she doing here? I don't want her to get too close. So I return his smile, shyly.

He strolls toward me, bows again and addresses me in French. 'Madame, surely your husband is an oaf, abandoning so charming a lady.'

I simper like a virgin in a romance novel. 'You are too kind, Herr Oberst.' Up closer, I see the threads of silver-grey and the lines around the eyes which gaze down at me. Pass him in the street, when he was out of uniform, you would take him for a bank manager, a prosperous businessman – or a doctor.

'Shall we walk, madame?' A brief lordly sweep of his arm encompasses the scene above the sea-lapped beach.

How can I refuse? The day chills momentarily; then I gather my wits. This may give us the opportunity we need. If I can get him near the photograph and then create some kind of diversion…

'With pleasure.' I see Adèle, who has been discreetly scanning the revellers, withdraw towards the kitchen. I take his arm and we proceed.

For some moments, silence. Then, just for something to say, I tell him I was a frequent visitor here, before the war.

The word drops like a stone between us. This man does not strike me as a fanatic. He must know that they have lost, that he is now engaged in a holding operation. The Allied armies have passed over our insignificant little island but they will be back, eventually. What waits for him then?

But he acknowledges none of this. Instead, I am taken on a botanical tour, complete with Latin names, guided around beds of irises, anemones and pinks. I contribute where I can, trying not to show that these domesticated flowers bore me. I prefer the succulents and cacti, so sexual and exuberant, which grow in our garden. Nevertheless, I smile and nod.

My escort tells me the Jersey climate and rainfall is similar to that of his native Bremen. With a boyish, self-deprecating smile, he says that his tulips and hyacinths have won prizes in that city's flower shows. 'But I'm sure you have your own fine garden, madame.'

I open my mouth to tell him about the cacti but then pull myself up short, laugh and say that we leave that to the local man we employ. – I confine myself to the interior. My husband sees to the outside.

'Indeed.' He regards me approvingly. I have given the correct answer.

I seize my chance. I touch his arm very lightly, somewhere between a pat and a caress. 'This has been a lovely tour but I wondered if I might see inside. I understand you have a fine photographic portrait by Heinrich Hoffmann.'

He looks a little surprised, but then nods and turns toward the entrance. 'Of course.'

We pass through the familiar doors where in 1937 Henri Michaux waited for Lucy and me, debonair in a dark suit, his crimson bow tie threaded with gold. Now, the reception desk is presided over by an unsmiling *fraulein* dressed in grey. Ahead is the staircase, wearing its crown.

As we ascend, I see framed by a window giving on to a back terrace Adèle's daughter holding court with some of the lower ranks. It is not just wartime deprivation which causes the shortness and tightness of her skirts. She smiles, tosses her head, accepts a cigarette. The table is well supplied with bottles of beer and schnapps.

'Bees around a honeypot,' my companion says. There is something unpleasant, almost prurient in the way he looks at Gabrielle, then he returns his gaze to me. 'You have children, madame?'

'No.' I affect an expression of suitably veiled distress. 'No, we weren't blessed.'

He regards me sympathetically. 'That must be a great sorrow for you. A woman can have no higher calling. My wife and I are expecting our eighth.'

I almost shriek, although whether this is the result of horror or mirth I can't say. The thought of the dutiful *frau*, methodically impregnated on every leave like a brood mare, or, to describe her using a more horticultural metaphor, this ever-blooming rose planted in fertile soil.

But I can only murmur, 'Indeed, God has smiled upon you.' (God smiled upon me when I had my hysterectomy; no more fainting, cramps and floods of monthly blood.)

There it is: the photograph of the madman attempting to look magisterial looms before us. Two guards salute. I see that there is no way to subvert this large square piece of kitsch. Its subtle hand-tinting gives it pretensions to a Renaissance masterpiece and there is an element of the frozen monumental quality one finds in a Piero della Francesca – but only an element. The subject is shown in profile, like a cardinal or an aristocrat, but neither cardinals nor aristocrats ever organised exhibitions of 'degenerate art' which drove painters to suicide. (Lucy wept when she heard that Kirchner had shot himself in Switzerland.)

Beside me, the flower grower looks suitably reverential. 'A great man.'

'A charismatic leader,' I murmur neutrally and see him glance at me, his face opaque.

We descend in silence. I try to imagine what he would say if he knew that beside him walked a pervert, a degenerate, someone who made the type of art crushed by the thug in the photo. What would he think about the paintings we own: Miro's carnivalesque fantasies, Picasso's dismemberment of reality?

But then all thoughts of art, of anything at all, disappear because, as we pass the windows and I look for the frivolous Gabriella, I see my husband, isolated as an island, being pincered between two Field Police. They stroll towards him, one on either side, until they snap their grey claws shut and force him down onto his knees. One of them contemptuously knocks off his hat, revealing the blonde fuzz beneath.

I gasp softly. The officer beside me, this gallant and pleasant progenitor, grasps my arm above the elbow, not brutal enough to leave a bruise but with sufficient strength to ensure my acquiescence. I think about twisting free and causing a scene, making bizarre accusations about his behaviour, anything to create a diversion; but it would be pointless. I cannot leave her. I am the shadow to her light, the electron which dances with her proton, the one seed of a dicotyledon which nestles next to the other. I cannot leave.

'This way, madame.'

They have timed our seizure well. People drift steadily away from the hotel, surfeited and chattering about the lovely afternoon. Even now, I want to open my mouth to scream, but who would aid us? If we managed to escape, there is any number who would assist in our recapture.

Over my shoulder, I glimpse Adèle Madec. She alone seems to realise what is happening as she stands there, staring. Perhaps she is the one: the betrayer.

They herd us, unhurried and unspeaking, towards the waiting black cars.

captivate

1944–1945

So, suddenly, in this dank fetid solitude, a lozenge of light opens. There is a gleam of hope which flutters down on paper normally used for wiping one's arse.

Well, we are not living in normal times.

I seize it, this twist of flimsy greyish stuff conveyed by its pulley of string along the shafts which carry the smell of shit and old vegetables.

…you are my air, my breath…

and then a drawing, a caricature, a voluptuous creature, mysteriously winged, no zephyr, but airborne nonetheless.

That's when I know that she is alive; that the poison we took has not destroyed her mind.

My cell, with its wafer mattress, its gruel-coloured blanket and its tarnished receptacle for shit, does not inspire me to nun-like gratitude. I do not sink to my knees to offer up thanks. Instead, I take the stub of pencil Otto found for me, along with my own private stash of crap-paper and scribble.

She made for herself a secret chamber on the roof of her house where she lived shut away… All the world proclaims that you are the only one whose power…and your military discipline is praised in all the nations.

I am praising her Judith, one of the Heroines she created when we lived free: for this is what I'm saying, that we will live free once more. I draw a woman crowned with a halo of hissing snakes dancing a tarantella. Underneath, I insert my own narrative: *Holofernes is just around the corner!* Then I fold my billet-doux until it is no bigger than a postage stamp. I settle on my bed, trying not to sleep. If there is nothing else with which to occupy your time, sleep, that lazy charmer, beckons seductively.

I try not to sleep, because now that time is filled with fragments of memory I suppress during my waking hours, the shards of black glass that rise from my unconscious. These are the memories of shouting and threats, of hard fingers poking my breastbone, just above the slope of soft flesh, of warnings, repeated, repeated, repeated, that they 'would make it very difficult for your families!' Then I was glad that we had been islands on this island.

This was when they still believed that we were part of some greater conspiracy, that there must be a whole spy network operating to undermine them. They wanted names.

'Information!' Oberst Samsen, my own captor, bellowed like a bull. '*Who* are they? *Where* are they?'

But we had nothing to give them, except the details of our own activities, which we freely supplied; after all, the past was past and there was nothing they, or anyone else, could do about it.

But still they pressed on, unbelieving, until we moved in a miasma of sleeplessness and the only release was the final sleep, the pills we had hidden, which were both sacrament and pact. They found us in our cells and in their hospital we returned, Lazarus-like, our breath stinking, limbs warmed once more with blood. I had such strange visions, when I walked in the land of the dead, saw creatures that even Bosch could not have dreamed: so now, I try not to sleep.

I sit on the bed, holding the grubby square like a talisman then thrust it hastily beneath my skirt when I hear footsteps made by the shiny black boots they wear. But this is no torturer. It is my friend Otto, bearing more crap paper and, I hope, news. I pass him the note, which he accepts with formal Prussian courtesy. His aberrant yellow hair shines, the one brightness in this grey light. (I have a childish craving for coloured crayons, to see scarlet and aqua and viridian, on a page.)

He looks around quickly then hands me a small and greasy parcel which only my impeccable training early in life prevents me from tearing open. In return, I give him my missive.

'Miss Schwob is well. She…'

'Is she eating?'

'We must all eat and, certainly, Miss Schwob is eating. Her food is eaten – if what we are served in here can be called food.'

Our laughter is as thin as the soup slopped into my metal bowl each day. That is mainly what we are given, plus dry stale bread. There is no letter but Otto assures me there will be one later. I ask him about Dieter, his friend, but his face closes over and he says nothing.

Left alone, I tear open the parcel then tear the chicken meat from the bone, gobbling. There is a wing and a thigh. The good Madame Rondel has been at work but where did she find this fine *poulet*? There are also a few olives and some pieces of tomato. I fantasise about fresh bread smothered in salty Jersey butter, cheese made from the milk of those same doe-eyed cows, meat-heavy stews, crème caramel… I throw the bones into the shit can and wipe my fingers.

The constant prison clamour, a bizarre strident music made up of shouted orders and obscenities, groans, stamping and clanging, has muted. Night must be coming on. I take the greasy paper, am about to ball it with my fist when I see the faint words pencilled: 'strength… steadfast…'; the remainder is indecipherable. I stare at them as though they are hieroglyphs from a lost civilisation. I think about keeping the paper but know that the smell will attract mice so throw it into the shit can, too. Something about these intermittent scratchings comforts me more than any food. Despite everything, I sleep and, for once, do not dream

Thunder wakes me. I rise, groggy and mishearing, thinking there must be soldiers near, then realise there is someone pounding on the floorboards. Staggering, taking one step then another, I haul up the loose slat of wood in the centre of the cell. A freckled white arm thrusts up, supporting a feral green eye. I feel great nostalgia for this unknown person; her disembodied parts always remind me of the art Lucy and I made for *Aveux non avenus*, so long ago. If I had a camera, I would record my anonymous neighbour; as it is, I take the note from her pale floating hand, thank her and slide the board shut.

She remembers! She answers me as Judith. She draws her, calm-faced, statuesque, confronting the brute. Where's the sword? Sneaky Judith! I can't see it. Beneath this cartoon there are some lines of scrawl, telling me about her neighbours. There is Karl who has deserted his country's army because he has seen the writing on the wall. (He has also seen the writing on some of our leaflets.) There is also Yosyp, a smutty Ukrainian joker, jovially salacious, even though he might be shot tomorrow for the crime of stealing from his captors. Yosyp has sworn vengeance to every German, including his fellow prisoners. He predicts rape and slaughter once the Red Army (which he also hates) reaches Berlin.

Otto has found out that Dieter is still alive. He is being held in A Block. He is suffering. They are both suffering…

I chew up the letter, slide it round my tongue as though I can feel her, taste her. I know what suffering means, although there are degrees, differences. They will have beaten Dieter, broken bones. He was stupid to have kept that photo of himself and a young man, taken at a fancy dress ball, somewhere, sometime, during those halcyon Weimar days. Pray that he does not give them Otto's name, for then our friend, our courier with the aberrant yellow hair, is doomed.

I pace up and down, like a tiger in a zoo cage. At times, her absence is like a wound; this is one of those times. Sticky August heat has penetrated even this clammy place. I itch and scratch. The shit stinks worse than usual. Restless, furious: I want to open my mouth to roar. Instead, I take out the pencil. I close my eyes and reach into memory.

A woman is on the move. Toward the camp of the conqueror!… but then I blank, can't think of anything courageous, something that will stop her mind veering towards the abyss. I hear footsteps, not high shiny black ones but the shuffle of padded leg wrappings. It's one of the slaves but not one I know or can trust, someone whose eyes and cheekbones tell me his home is on the steppe riding a half-wild pony. For one mad moment, I imagine overpowering him, smashing his face into the floorboards and fleeing. But it passes, if for no other reason than I have no wish to hurt him, this man with sores on his mouth and hair stiffened with grime.

At the door he hesitates, holding the foul can, then turns and tells me in soft, broken German that some of the mad dictator's peers have tried to kill him. 'They gone…finished…'

He mimes a cut throat, even though I doubt that this is the way 'they' have been 'finished'. I ask him for numbers, names, but he shakes his head. Gossip swirls and eddies in this place; it is easy to be carried along on a tide of half-truths and speculation, only to be washed up on a beach of despair due to some optimist's misinformation. Nevertheless, I include it in my letter: 'some of the inner circle has turned full circle so it can only be a matter of time…'

The question for us is, will there be enough time?

November 1944

The morning of our trial. I would like to array myself like an antique heroine, Cleopatra in many-coloured silks or Mary Queen of Scots, jewelled velvet and lace. Instead, I dress in the grey and beige clothes worn to rags, my dingy uniform of confinement.

First, they see us separately. I am shown to the now-familiar room but today there are three: Bohde, Lohse, as well as Samsen. The big guns: Bohde, highest ranked, although you would not guess it if you saw all three without uniform. His nose has been broken, probably more than once, and this, together with thin shoulders and a chest which is almost concave, give him a slightly misaligned look, as though the parts do not fit well. (How did he make it into the Field Police? Family connections? Ideological zeal?)

If Lohse was not intelligent, he would just be a thug; as it is, he is a sadist, a predator, someone who has found a natural home in this regime. He has a fleshy handsome face and thick dark hair. No doubt many women find him attractive. He is the one who opens the proceedings, once I am seated. I expect the well-worn questions about accomplices, my mind already preparing answers mechanically, like wheels fitting into a deep-rutted road. But I am in for a surprise.

'What is the exact nature of your relationship to your fellow defendant, Lucy Schwob?'

'You know that already. We are sisters.'

Lohse stares at me. He leers slightly. 'When we arrested the other defendant, she was dressed as a man.'

'My sister is an actress.' I meet his gaze.

'Really?' He rises and, despite a fidget of discomfort from Bohde, walks around the table at which they are seated and approaches. He hovers. He smiles at me, as though he has some special knowledge. I imagine him during the Weimar years, sitting in a darkened theatre watching a live sex show, two women paid to fuck each other so their children could eat.

'She was an actress in Paris.' I stare back unflinchingly. Why should I not? It is entirely true. 'Life for her is theatre. She loves dressing up. She is like a child.'

He looms so close that I can smell his sweat, hear his breathing. For a moment, I think he will do something violent or obscene; then he collects himself and walks away.

'It does not matter if you are perverts or mere decadents. You are both going to die.'

Bohde calls him to heel. Their questions become the familiar ones. Always I remain steadfast in my answers. For this, I am threatened with transfer to the dreaded A Block, where the food is less and worse and it is rumoured that the guards make Lohse look like a kindergarten teacher. (Perhaps there are kindergarten teachers like Lohse. Perhaps that is what is wrong with the world.)

Finally, I am escorted outside. And she is there! For the first time in four months: the beloved visage. When the food did not come, or when there was not enough to nourish me, there have been moments of head-spinning whiteness when her face disappeared. This was when I reached real despair. But now, here she is.

Privation has sharpened her body to a blade. The air parts for her. My eyes trace the curve of her nose, touch the soft flesh remaining beneath her jaw. I want to hold her, feel my mouth on hers.

As it is, I raise one hand, my face calm and smiling slightly. 'Sister, are you well?'

The guard barks at us to be quiet but for several precious minutes before they take her into the room we are left on the bench outside with a guard at each end of the corridor. She gazes at me, unseeing. Her eyes have the sheen of glass. My tendril of hope, that her sanity remains untouched, withers.

'I've been talking to Henri. He has so much to tell me.'

She believes Michaux is speaking to her. Well, why not? I decide to treat the whole thing as a game and enter into it.

'What does he say? Is he well?' And then I hear about the funnels of drug-dreams down which he disappears and the mad poetry born of these excursions. She is convinced that Michaux is living in a tree in Buenos Aires with a view which stretches to the edge of the pampas. Well, why not? I ask her to recite the poetry but she claims he has sworn her to silence.

'Ssshhh! It's a secret.'

Then suddenly her mind clears and she returns to me. She asks about my time with Bohde, Lohse and Samsen. I tell her about Lohse's prediction, that death in imminent for us both. That's when she reveals that she still has some pills.

She whispers, 'Let us not give them the satisfaction. Let us die together. We will be Romeo and Juliet, Tristan and Isolde, Siegfried and Odette, twinned in our desire for final union.'

I see that she is in love with this idea. Very well. The Allies have forsaken our island. If we are not killed by the Germans, it will be slow starvation in A Block or a long train ride through a wrecked and smoking Europe to a camp.

'Let there be no letters,' I tell her. 'There will be no message written down. Our lifeless bodies will be the message.'

By the end of the afternoon they have found us guilty. They tell us we are to be killed for the crime of propaganda and that we are to serve a further six months in prison for listening to the BBC and possessing the camera and gun.

'Do we serve the six months before or after our execution?' I ask Samsen.

'Silence!' roars that mild-mannered hyacinth grower. Is it my imagination or do I see Bohde's thin lips twitch?

It is not difficult to get Yosyp to procure a kitchen knife. I fast, refuse even the few revolting morsels he brings me on a plate and then cut quickly and deep. It hardly hurts. Scarlet rivulets trickle, slowly at first then gather strength. I lie on the bed and drift away, carried out on a tide of memory…

…there is Henri, smiling crookedly as he leans against a crumbling arch of medieval stone… Lucy has her camera…

…　　　　　…　　　　　…　　　　　…

she has her camera…she stands on the beach… Henri smiles…

…　　　　　…　　　　　…　　　　　…

…the beach at Jersey…somebody

　　　　　somebody　　　　a little girl in dark bloomers…

…　　　　　…　　　　　…　　　　　…

…　　　　　…　　　　　…　　　　　…

my mother calls me…she's getting married… 'Monsieur Schwob…'
Lucy　　　　　she swings from the café trellis, face alight

Lucy

she has her camera　　　　　Sylvia Beach
she's just opened her bookshop　　　looks proud…in the photo

André　　　　　Jacqueline
…　　　　　…　　　　…

Lucy

    ...

Lucy

  ...   ...

Lucy

...   .

February 1945

Finally, they have allowed us a cell together. On the third day, they unwound our grave cloths and we rose transcendent, streaming with light. For some time, our mouths opened and shut (but emitted no words) and our eyes stared back at *the flat stone of a symbolically empty tomb*; then we returned to the world.

Perhaps they thought it was a miracle; perhaps they could not be bothered with us any more. This slightly larger enclosure has a tiny window at the top of one wall and at night we curl together on one of narrow beds and try to count the stars. So far, we are up to three. Hours pass. The worst of the winter is over but the cold still gnaws. Sometimes she murmurs drowsily, repeats fragments of the intense philosophical discussions she held with Michaux. I myself can recall nothing of that time. It is a blank of darkness.

But now, in this time of darkness, we marry each other, a blasphemy of which our captors remain mercifully ignorant. Messages still come to us via the ventilation shafts (which still carry the smell of shit). In this way, Feral Eye is revealed as Marie, a maid in one of the island's big houses, who has been caught with a copy of an English newspaper and promptly turned in by her employer. It is Marie who tells us that we have missed our train to the East, that it left the station while we wallowed near death. *'Rumour has it that there will be no more...'*

Well...

We know how unreliable Rumour can be; we shall wait and see what else he has to say. Yosyp seems to have disappeared but Rumour is silent about this.

Buried in an unmarked grave? Transferred to another block? Rumour's mouth is taped. We know that our friend Otto, whose beacon hair is dulled and whose lips are cracked and bleeding, has retreated into silence, will not look at us, let alone speak. Lucy puts one hand through the bars but he turns away.

In the days that follow, one after the other, broken beads clacking slowly down a string, nothing changes except that the food parcels, which continue to arrive from Madame Rondel, contain less and less. There is a cold roast potato which we devour greedily; half a turnip and a few legumes which we soften in our mouths. The whole island battles to survive the Allies' negligence, the wilful push ahead which has left us still ensnared. (We hear – Rumour has passed this along the ventilation telegraph – that things are not much better in France, but at least there they are free.) Always our housekeeper exhorts us to courage and tells us she remembers us in her prayers.

'Let us hope she is not praying to St Jude.'

Lucy lies on the bed opposite. Her eyes are closed; her breathing barely swells her chest. It is difficult to be courageous when you are subsisting on half your normal kilojoule requirement. It is difficult to be courageous when the person you love more than your life tells you she hears Henri Michaux reciting his new poetry: *There is not one self/ There are not ten selves/ There is no self.* Is this what she wants, still: *no self?* But then she shifts, rolls onto her side and fixes me with her blue untrammelled gaze, tells me that, lying in hospital, she decided to live when she heard that I had survived.

'I could not leave you to face them alone.'

Hearing this, and knowing it is true, it is still difficult to be courageous when we are summoned before our interrogators again; nevertheless, we stand quietly and listen to the reprieve. We are not to be killed, not yet. We are not to be put on a train. The last train has gone. (German trains always run on time.) Several important men (is the Baron one of them?) have rallied to our cause. No, merely if we repent of our sins, we will be forgiven…

Well, not quite. We are to most humbly protest our innocence and appeal our sentence.

No.

This is when she tells them that her father was a Jew.

'You did not register this fact, madame.'

'No, but I would not have registered being a member of the Salvation Army either.'

Her questioner scowls. His job has just been made more difficult and he does not like it. Abruptly, he tells us to leave, that we will be summoned again soon.

We are close to the door when she collapses. Falls down as though dead. I see an expression of exasperation cross Bohde's face. What a nuisance we are! He summons the guard and Otto approaches, assists her to her feet and supports her to the cell. He denies her any medication (they all know what can happen with that) but brings her cold water and a cloth. It is when he is sponging her face that he tells us that Dieter is dead, shot as 'a traitor to the race'. Through all his terrible time before, he refused to give up another name. Otto and another man took the body away where it was buried without a headstone.

'At least I did not have to do the killing.'

At this, Lucy cries out. I think back to the questions they asked me about my sister who likes to dress up. They must have wondered about us, suspected. Strange that they did not ask her; perhaps my own performance was convincing.

I turn back to Otto. 'You must try to live for Dieter, live for him, despite what they did.'

'What would you know about it, you…' Then he calls us a foul name.

Lucy flinches. I stare at him steadily but he offers no apology, no word at all. After he leaves, we sit together, the blankets around us, trying to keep warm.

'He hates us for surviving.'

'He hates himself for not being able to protect his lover.'

For the next few days, she withdraws, barely speaks. She fasts, although this is barely possible on our dreadful rations. I fight my own lethargy, the terrible dragging weariness starvation induces. It is so tempting to take flight too; but one of us must remain.

But one morning she takes up the pencil she still has with her and begins to write our story. Each morning, if she is not too weak, she writes. She writes, sitting on the bed, propped against the wall, occasionally lifting her eye to the slit of light the window allows. Her 'Testament' pours out. When she tells Otto, he says nothing but later returns with a stash of paper which he says has come from Lohse's office. Sublime irony! She writes on.

Our captors summon us repeatedly, always wanting us to plead our innocence. We refuse. We own to everything we have done. If we die, we die with this knowledge.

When her breathing shortens and she has to lay aside her pencil, I take over and she dictates. Sometimes she is unable to do even that and lies on the bed, eyes closed. Then I can only wait, sit beside her and rest my hand on her forehead.

'Suzanne…my mirror…my other self…'

When I look down, I see myself reflected in the dark pupils the blue iris surrounds like a sea.

We give excerpts of the 'Testament' to Otto, who takes them away. When he reads the first, something like a smile touches his face. A tear runs down one cheek. He looks at her. 'Is it worth the price, to bear witness to this time?'

'It must be.'

Later, he returns to tell us that our home has been raped, that there are paintings gone, clothes flung from cupboards, furniture overturned, vile things scrawled on the walls. Someone has made a fire in the garden; in the litter of ash, there remain fragments of glass and paper.

When Lucy hears this, she does not break down, as I fear, just takes up the pencil and continues. I tell Otto to bury the 'Testament' beneath the largest cactus, the one which riots into mauve and magenta flowers.

I tell him where the gardening tools are kept, if they have not been stolen too. It should be possible to dig quickly, for spring is coming. The stars in the window burn with a softer light although the night air still cuts to the bone. If the Germans decide on their final solution for us, then someone will know where to find our words.

We are still on thin ice. We must reach the other side before the thaw.

8 May 1945

The English major approaches us almost diffidently. 'Oh, ladies… I had no idea there was anyone else left.'

Lucy smiles and holds out her hand. 'We are real. We are not ghosts.'

Well…

It has been easy these last few days, as they all left, one after the other, to feel as though we existed in limbo, neither ether nor earth, that freedom was just a chimera but here is the major, square, solid, an altogether splendid chap in his neatly pressed khaki and bright cap badge. He is so pleasant and friendly as he summons an underling to release us and then escorts us along the damp grey corridor. Once, Lucy stumbles and he puts one hand beneath her elbow and brushes away her apology. He is courteous, solicitous, but does not pay much attention to our claim that some of the guards were human and sought to make our situation easier. I wonder where Otto is (there is still no sign of Yosyp) and what has happened to Bodhe, Lohse and Samsen.

'You have to sign some papers,' the major tells us.

Of course, of course we must sign papers. How else to make our liberation complete? We are taken to the same room where we have so often stood but this time chairs are provided as well as military issue stationery. I think of the toilet paper we used, which was part of our desperate survival, and begin to laugh softly. The major glances at me sharply, annoyed. He does not want an insane woman on his hands, not at this stage, when the mopping up is almost complete.

We sign what we have to sign; the words are irrelevant. Now we must face what lies outside, in bright sunshine.

We blink like subterranean animals emerging from hibernation as the wind whips at us, blowing our hair and skirts. From her meagre bundle of possessions, Lucy takes a headscarf, improbable in its gauziness, and ties it beneath her chin. I tease her, tell her it makes her look like an old babushka, and she pokes out her tongue. Before us is the broad spread of grass, seen only once when we were taken here nine months ago and, on the other side, the high barred gate. There is a figure, waiting, but we cannot make out who it is. We wish for Henri, we wish for André and Jacqueline; perhaps someday... In the distance, there is our old friend, the glinting sea. Lucy turns up her face to the light, raises her arms and smiles.

As we begin to cross the grass, eyed only by a few uncurious soldiers, there is a shout and the sound of running feet.

'Get back, Kraut!' someone snarls and there is Otto, dishevelled but at least clean now, with his chapped lips healed and his hair once more bright as money.

I hold up my hand to the belligerent tommy in a gesture intended to be at once commanding and pacifying. 'Please, this man is our friend.'

He shrugs and turns away. We are just a pair of old women and no concern of his. Otto stops short, formal and constrained. We expect him to click his heels.

'I apologise, for the bad things I said...'

Impulsively I embrace him, tell him he has known great sorrow, call him our brother.

He looks embarrassed, draws back gently and extends the things he is holding, the pieces of fabric which curl like birds, to Lucy. 'Take them. I don't want them. I won't need them any more.' They are the badges from his tunic and others which must come from a dress uniform. 'Keep them, to remember me.'

Lucy removes her scarf, wraps them and places them carefully in her bundle. 'What will happen to you now?'

'I don't know,' then he adds, as a postscript to his own history, 'always, the men of my family are in the army.'

We wish to speak more but by now the English are upon him. The last we see is the yellow hair pushed down roughly by a clamping hand, the holes made in the victors' faces as they jeer and curse.

But these are drowned by a distant roar, louder than the sea. Through the streets there surges a tidal wave of people, liberated islanders rejoicing.

'I want to join them!'

'No,' I tell her, reinstating our ancient battle with one word. 'If we go anywhere, it will be to the hospital, to have you cared for.'

Also, but I do not say this, *the joy of a crowd has a thousand mouths – and no ears.* The mob can crush, the mob destroys; it is so easy to get swept up, swirled off your feet and lose your mind so that exhilaration becomes obliteration. Torchlight procession; victory parade: beware of them both.

She follows me in sullen silence across the gently sloping grass, still longing for the annihilation of anonymity. I grasp her hand, leading her forward firmly as the still figure ahead takes on form and substance: Adèle Madec, waiting for us at the gates.

liberté

1945

For it was Adèle all along: so she tells us during our slow journey towards home (still no cars for civilians), making our way through people thronging to St Helier to celebrate. We push back against this river rushing to the sea, periodically stopping to rest on some convenient low fence or public seat. Lucy's breath labours; I stumble once. Relief at our survival mingles with apprehension about what we will find, a feeling not eased by the details of our companion's story. Farm in Normandy laid waste during World War I, husband killed at Ypres, son killed at Cambrai: a lifelong hatred for the Krauts.

'So when I arrived on this island and was approached by the British, wanting to know if I could be "useful", I was very happy to oblige.'

I nod, almost absent-mindedly. Nothing surprises me now. I find I have no interest in the woman's activities. They are all past tense, slipping into the great sludge of history. My eye traces the curve of the bay, loving the waves' opalescent lustre, knowing that this alone continues, with the sun and the wind and the seasons. In the distance, I see Noirmont Point, with the grey observation tower thrusting skywards, built to last one thousand years. I help Lucy to her feet.

'We thought it was our housekeeper who was helping keep us alive.'

'That *pétainiste!* Adèle scoffs. 'Likely she was keeping tabs on you and probably informed…'

'No! She is a loyal and honest woman!' Lucy cuts her off, her face white.

Adèle subsides. I see a gleam of pity for our gullibility. She seems to judge the world by harsh, unforgiving standards. Despite her kindness to us, I'm not sure I want this woman for a friend. But she offers us small pieces of bread and cheese to sustain us on our journey and I'm grateful.

'You know there has been food and medicine on the island since the end of last year,' and Adèle tells us about the *Vega*, sent with Red Cross supplies after Churchill was finally made to give up his iron embargo. We saw none of it; the starving frantic Germans kept whatever they could obtain for themselves.

We reach the edge of the plateau which hugs St Aubin's Bay and begin our descent, guided by the benevolent west-sinking sun. Walking through the narrow, stonewalled lanes there is absolute quiet, broken by the sound of our footsteps and the breathing I know Lucy is trying to suppress. A blanket of reed warblers lifts from a field beneath the chalky sky. I have a sudden feeling of disorientation; if it were not for Adèle's presence, I could believe it was a day in the late thirties, when all that was to come was just a slumbering nightmare.

But as we enter the nest of streets behind the St Brelade's Bay hotel a young woman approaches, her lumpy figure enhanced by the turquoise cashmere shawl she's wrapped it with. She's not someone we know, I think, confused by the sight of Lucy's shawl; but then recognition dawns: it's the same dumpy pasty girl we saw so long ago, gazing adoringly at her very own *ubermensch* as they stood near the wall built by slaves.

Rage flames through me. I block her path and seize her arm. 'Give that back! It's not yours! Give it back right now!'

But she merely smiles and shakes me off, as though I was a troublesome insect.

'Give it back!' I push her, quite hard.

Suddenly I want to kill this smug bitch who has desecrated our lives by her thievery. I slap her across the face. People have come out of the shops to watch but before I can go any further Lucy pulls me away.

'Leave it be. I don't want it any more.' She speaks quietly; her glance wills away the woman who finally has the grace to look shamefaced before continuing down the street.

A man shakes his head, smiling slightly at this catfight, and returns to his counter in the pharmacy. The village goes about its business. Adèle, who has taken no part in this fracas – perhaps she doesn't want to alienate customers – walks along beside us, unperturbed.

Dusk is settling by the time we reach the house. The melancholy pall that this time of day sometimes engenders now seems quite kind, a necessary filter for the vandalism and disarray which await us. However, there is one glorious surprise. As we approach the house, open the side gate and walk along the path, Mignonette runs to meet us. Lucy picks up the old cat, cradling her in her arms and crooning. I stroke the calico fur and sing praises to her survival.

Adèle stands apart, pleased by our pleasure but uncomprehending as to why we would expend it on this gaunt and shabby creature. 'I tried to find your other one but...he disappeared.'

I shudder. I know what 'disappeared' means, that our poor Tiger, that pathetic tabby, became a feline sacrifice, some malnourished islander's dinner. But we are so please to see Mignonette that that night she sleeps between us on the impromptu bed we construct in the living room, for we cannot bear to enter the bedroom, even though the worst of the damage is gone and the anti-Semitic obscenities have been sloppily painted over. But we feel them, pentimento, breathing behind the mask, so we pile rugs on the living room floor then heap the blankets on top. Candles cast shadows which flicker and loom, shapes comforting in their grotesquery. We are in a cave, back where time began and the mind and body were free to play. On the edge of exhaustion, I hold her, listen to the low hiss of her breath, hope beyond all hope that the sea and the sun will heal her.

'We must get another,' she murmurs drowsily, 'but not until Mignonette...'

'Hush, enough, she mustn't hear...'

It is in the morning, in the stark light of day that we see the blank spaces on the walls. Our cheeky little Miro is gone and the two Picasso sketches, the Max Ernst oil and Leonor Fini's wild self-portrait. Vases have been smashed and posters defaced. Adèle has left a supply of food and we breakfast on bread and chicory coffee but when Lucy sees the full devastation wrought upon our photographs, she vomits abruptly and runs from the room. I clean up the mess then turn my attention to what is left but there is little to be saved: a few empty file boxes, paper packets, bearing the name of the local pharmacy, which hold some negatives but no prints. I pick one up from the floor and hold it to the light: there we are, both in swimming costumes, languishing on the low stone fence at the bottom of the garden which overlooks the beach. I place it in one of the paper envelopes, sink to my hands and knees and crawl around the floor, looking for anything to salvage.

Thus it is that Adèle finds me when she returns, arse facing her, blood rushing to my cheeks as I rise. But she knows better than to intrude into this sanctum.

She tells me Lucy is asleep, that she has organised several men to repaint the most damaged rooms. She carries a woven basket over one arm. 'It's too early to do much pruning but I'll help you with weeding.'

The garden is an overgrown shambles and there is a ragged round mark in the garden, like a lesion or a scar, where the fire has been. I see shards of glass singed black, shrivelled twists of acetate, the detritus of destruction. We work side by side, bent over like peasants in a Millet painting, freeing the plants from encroachment.

Sweat runs freely. We stop to rest and Adèle brings out a pitcher of water and glasses. She mentions rumours of wild scenes in St Helier the previous night, jubilation spilling over into orgy and excess, bare-breasted women waving to soldiers from balconies. Such stories about these sedate earthbound people stretch my credulity. I glance sideways at her, unbelieving then finish our water and resume. The sun strikes striations of light from the waves. I remember the grey November day Lucy and I bought the Miro for Henri, bidding at auction against some portly little man wearing pince-nez but Henri saw how much Lucy loved it and gave it back to her. 'You take it, dear heart. I can easily hallucinate Miro.'

Now lost forever to some private collection in Berlin.

Adèle has brought real baguettes for lunch and half a cold chicken. There's some pre-war Muscadet and a few small apples. We eat with en-

joyment, hungry after our labour but Lucy, roused from sleep, wrapped
in a blanket, picks at a shred of white flesh then accepts a sliver of fruit.
Later, she sits on the lawn in a high-backed rattan chair and supervises
us. Adèle and I make jokes, call her 'slave-driver' and 'plantation owner'.
There she sits, my battered princess, turning her puffy face to the sun,
brown-spotted hands idle in her lap. Her eyes gaze with seemingly va-
cant indifference at our surroundings yet it is she who spots the Baron
deep in conversation with British officers on the steps of the hotel.

'Our hero,' I say, half-believing it, thinking of the powerful men
who spoke up for us in prison.

Adèle snorts. 'Be very careful which prince you choose,' and then
goes on to tell us how very happily the Baron received the Germans in
his home, how he had even assisted them by providing the names of
certain persons who then disappeared. 'Sent them to camps, that's what
your hero did. And now he's covering his tracks, cuddling up to the
British, who probably won't do anything about it anyway. It's likely he
is the one who turned you in. Believe me, he didn't suffer – his good
friends always made sure he had plenty to eat.'

I glance at Lucy, to see how she has responded to these accusations
but she is watching a distant figure moving along the beach and appears
to have taken no notice of what's been said. I keep my eyes on the dark
soil and pluck and hoe, thinking how this woman, Adèle, could hold a
grudge until the end of time. I sense her resentment, even bitterness
against the British, those who she undertook to serve and who then vir-
tually abandoned her. As for the Baron, well…anything is possible. He
may have felt that he was protecting people when he befriended the invaders.

On the other hand, the Baron was present on the fateful day Lucy
and I were arrested. Did he pierce our disguises then inform on us?
There is a tangle of ambiguity about these events which defeats me, and
hearsay, fuelled by speculation, can lead only to paranoia.

I sigh and watch the figure on the beach, listing slightly from side
to side, draw closer.

'Your daughter,' Lucy remarks quietly, and yes, it's Gabriella but not the laughing flirtatious minx that I've always seen.

Her sweater has been half-torn off. Weals lace her shoulders and her hair has been cropped but not shaved. There's a shallow bloody scrape above her left ear where a razor has sheared down to the scalp. She throws herself against her mother, who flinches slightly as she receives the weight then stands, rock steady and unspeaking while the girl makes guttural bleating sounds and beats her fists. I see that she is angry and humiliated but not broken: another survivor. I look at Lucy, who looks toward the house but Adèle catches our intention.

'Stay.'

It does not feel like a command to disobey; however, Lucy takes charge and shepherds us inside, makes tea, some strange herbal brew she has always claimed is helpful for her insomnia, then settles our guests on a couch.

The story comes out as we sip the pale, rather musty tea. A group of middle-aged people, mainly women, waylaid Gabriella, wanting to punish her for her 'friendship' with enemy soldiers. There is no rule of law; these people, probably all quiescent and servile during the war, now seek easy targets as an outlet for their guilt.

'But I got away. I kicked one of the old bitches in the…' the girl uses the crudest expression for a woman's private parts, '…and ran.'

As we laugh, I glance at Adèle. This fanatical German-hater, surely she could not have approved of her daughter's behaviour?

She turns her head slightly and meets my eyes. She smiles slightly, mockingly and then I see. I understand. I feel shock, a kind of disgust, at a woman who would pimp her own daughter, use her sexually to gain information. My hands tremble as I suggest quietly that Gabriella lie down for a while, for I know that, despite all her bravado, the girl is near collapse. And indeed, when she stands, she almost falls and I have to lead her to the besmirched bedroom, where I leave her to undress. When I open the door five minutes later, she is already asleep. A tiny transparent orb crowns the gentle swell of her cheek.

I go to find lavender oil so that I can bathe her wounds when she wakes then walk through the room where Lucy and Adèle converse, surrounded by empty teacups. I do not want to be near Adèle. There is something ugly, dirty, here. Nevertheless, she comes to find me, standing at the bottom of the garden, looking out at the sea.

'It is not for you to judge. Sometimes we do what is needed. Gabriella had a choice. At least there was no child.'

I think of the pale nape, naked to the world; the self-righteousness of those who did nothing to aid their own freedom but are now so quick to judge the ones who did. Away to my right in the distance is the observation tower at La Corbière. How long will it take the ocean to corrode the concrete? Hundreds of years? Thousands?

I turn tired, unforgiving eyes to Adèle. 'You are welcome to stay here until Gabriella can go home with you,' and as I say this, something shifts. I see, that through an act of kindness to this fractured woman and her injured daughter, Lucy and I redeem our house, that it ceases to be a place of desolation but becomes instead refuge and sanctuary so I have much reason to be grateful to Adèle, who nevertheless refuses my offer.

'Thank you but I will leave her resting with you and return tomorrow.'

We go back indoors, where she collects her basket then takes her leave.

'Strange,' I murmur to Lucy, as I sit down and lean into her.

She wraps me in her arms. 'The mother/daughter relationship is complex and sometimes not to be fathomed.'

She, who never knew her own mother: if Victorine had been sane, how much different would things have been? As I drift to sleep, I think of the triumphant, gloating faces of women with razors and hanks of hair in their hands; some part of their cruelty must have been founded in sexual jealousy, the wish to be desired, wanted, a captor's prize...

Violence, callousness, the murk of suspicion and doubt: is this what we have lived to inherit?

fantôme

1947

She still will not eat.

The glitter of the bubbles lures her. She relishes the slow slide of the liquid down her throat. The glass becomes a sacrament; its brittle sparkle consecrates her longing for health and work. For three days now, she has wandered, sleepless, while I trailed her with morsels, beseeching. Then last night, I abandoned this strategy, stalked off and left her as she scribbled dementedly to Breton. (Most nights now, she writes: to Breton, to Michaux, to Ernst and other ghosts from our past.)

Call off the pursuit, I thought, and left the food on the kitchen table, two slices of fresh tomato arranged on white cheese, a very small salad of greens and herbs. It's a delicious feast for a midget, perhaps one of Snow White's dwarves, but not for a healthy woman.

The doctor has said 'rich, nourishing food', well…let him try to make her eat, she who wants to live on the elixir of the grape. Let him trawl the shops and market, replenished now that the invaders have gone (but still not approaching the levels of pre-war bounty) seeking out vegetables and meat. At least now there is Adèle with her yard of chickens to replace Monsieur Rondel's rabbits (the Rondels long gone to Paris). But Lucy disdains even this harvested flesh, seeks instead aerial transcendence which, day after day, takes her to the wall below.

For she believes that she can fly. She has written to Breton that, feather-light, she will cross the water to him, float like mist, drift like spray, ethereal as bubbles rising through wine.

So I watch her through the window, see her poised precariously atop the row of stone with the waves, calm today, behind her. Her light-coloured skirt reaches her knees. Tucked into her belt is a swath of diaphanous fabric through which her breasts, still full despite her weight loss, are visible. In her right hand she carries a shepherd's crook. Who does she think she is? Little Bo Beep? She treads the wall as gracefully as a cat but I know if she falls there will be lacerations, blood. She is no sprite, no bodiless wisp of vapour. Someone has to catch her when she loses balance.

I put some plasters in the pocket of my skirt. I take my calm enfolding steadiness, which I try to put round her like a cloak. I also take the camera. As I cross the lawn, I gaze at her face dispassionately, as though seeing it for the first time. It is old now, seamed, incongruous above the flimsy attire but the eyes, which have seen so much, lend her an appearance of gravitas which saves her from derision. She balances, leans into the breeze, holds the end of the fabric out above her shoulder, making a gauzy wing. She is a bizarre divine, the fairy sent to confer mixed blessings at a ceremony of bats and sugar cakes.

Click! Click!

I press the shutter. Click! Again.

'Ah, Suzanne,' says a voice from the bottom of the steps which lead up to the gate. 'You are always the acolyte, never the angel.'

And there is Adèle with Gabriella and Raphael, who is snarling and snivelling, his blond curly hair giving him the appearance of a psychotic cherub. Despite the fractious child, his grandmother has taken in the whole scenario. She speaks ironically yet, as usual, skewers the truth. She assists Lucy down from the wall and we move inside, Raphael threatening to disrobe Lucy with sticky grasping hands. She laughs. There is something about her which a two-year-old finds irresistible. By the time we reach the house, his tantrum is entirely forgotten.

I set out the tea things; we are having tea in the English style, for which Adèle provides a plump fruit cake and scones. There is jam with joy! joy! joy! precious Jersey butter and cream. Gabriella sets to the weekly dusting and mopping while her mother coaches the child to drink milk and eat half a scone, which soon smears his mouth with jam and cream. Lucy places the other half on her plate and reduces it to crumbs with a fork while she drinks a cup of tea and looks longingly towards the kitchen, where Adèle has left the bottle of Pommery.

We hear the sound of running water as Gabriella begins cleaning the bathroom. Her hair is longer now and her clothes more sombre; since her son's birth, she has almost become a sensible young matron. The time she does not spend working in her mother's restaurant she engages in this kind of domestic employment in other houses besides ours. We are grateful for her services because since the war some kind of taint or stain seems to adhere to Lucy and me. Some people avert their eyes in the street; others who once greeted us cordially now do not. Our past activities have not won us respect, rather the reverse: we are seen as troublemakers who jeopardised the lives of ordinary, law-abiding citizens. So people avoid us, in all kinds of ways, which is why we value Gabriella. Even Adèle will sometimes lend a hand, taking away urine-soaked sheets to the laundry, although I also resent this assistance and the dependence we now have on them both.

For the war has taken its own toll on me, too. I am not as strong as I once was. I need them.

I pour more tea and cut the cake. Adèle begins on the local gossip, telling us that moves are afoot to reinstitute the annual Battle of the Flowers, the festival held on Jersey, complete with its parade of pretty girls on floats.

'Not all pretty girls,' interjects Lucy. 'You must remember in 1939, not long after Neville Chamberlain's appeasement speech, there was a float featuring Hitler, Mussolini and Franco…'

'Ah, yes,' I murmur, 'those great lovers of peace.'

'I remember.' Adèle's lips twist briefly. 'Your friend caused a minor scandal by shouting abuse at them as they passed.'

She's referring to Michaux, who didn't actually shout abuse but ran alongside the float as his alter ego, Plume, alternatively grovelling and catcalling, 'Oh, sirs! Kind sirs! When are you going to take over the world?' He was lucky he wasn't locked up. He did get pelted with someone's half-eaten apple and told to go back to Russia.

'Who might it be on the float next time?' Lucy's face wears a musing look as she watches Raphael busy with a set of blocks and toy train which once belonged to her brother. 'Will it be Eisenhower? de Gaulle? Stalin?'

We laugh and speculate.

Adèle says that our old friend, the Baron, has been particularly active in planning festival activities. 'Perhaps he's just seeking to turn the clock back, rather than wind it forward. Or perhaps he thinks that if he contributes enough to island affairs, people will forgive and forget.'

Adèle is overstating. Very few people appear to hold any grudge against this man. Most want to erase the bad years, continue as before and behave as though nothing has happened. Bread and circuses; flowers and floats. We see him occasionally, this Baron, and he is always courteous, always polite, raising his hat and smiling as he passes in company with his wife, she of the long nose and ashy marcelle wave. See how perfectly groomed the Baron is: nothing sticks to his handmade tweeds, no speck of dust or lint. Whatever nasty rumour regarding collaboration or assisting in the deportation of people to their death, he flicks it off then carefully bushes his lapels. He is still the gentleman, living the life to which he was born.

'His time will come,' I say, but as I speak I know that bad deeds often go unpunished and that retribution can remain a dream. It is easier to give yourself over to helping Adèle plan a menu or watch her grandson scatter coloured blocks with a petulant cry.

Lucy exits briefly and returns wearing a featureless white mask and making monster noises. The child squeals in delighted terror, runs out into the garden with Lucy in pursuit, just as his mother emerges from the kitchen peeling gloves from her hands.

After she has been paid and eaten a slice of cake, she and her mother collect Raphael and I watch them pass through the cemetery and linger briefly before one of the graves. Adèle places her hand upon the child's head. How she hated the idea of being grandmother to a bastard child of a Boche, but she seems to have come around, although I sometimes see her gaze at the child as though he's a changeling. Gabriella's son was born near the end of the liberation year; she must have already been carrying him during her time with us; her trauma and distress must have been compounded by the thought of her mother's displeasure.

Is this soldier entombed beneath Jersey soil the father? I can't ask. I don't.

I gather up the tea things and carry them to the sink. Lucy is quiet, preoccupied, then goes to find her writing materials. She has embarked upon a project to record our prison experiences but when she sits down at the long oak table in the dining room I see that she has the small blue notepaper used for letters, not a rough pad of foolscap. Outside, the sun has sunk beneath the waves and turned the rolling blue to antique grey. Gulls wheel and call on their way home. Occasional distant footsteps sound in the street.

I switch on the lamps and stand at the window. Cold gold light floods the room. The world feels weightless, static, out of time, although I know it changes every second. I glance at Lucy, her head bent as she covers the page. Perhaps she writes to Breton, who has returned to Paris with another wife while Jacqueline has remained in America with a new man. André says 'come'; Michaux says 'come'; all our old friends call to us across the Channel, assuring us there is a place for us, still.

Lucy yearns for it, talks constantly of renting a house on the Île de la Cité but I know what the doctor says: 'Plenty of rest, limited exertion'; so, for the moment, just these letters. Perhaps later, the boat to St Malo and then the train beyond; perhaps not.

Now the lights from the boats out on St Brelade's Bay gleam like specks of mica. I turn away from the window and ask whether she would like a simple omelette. She makes no reply. Chou-chou, our new black and white, brought to replace Mignonette, has returned now that the guests have gone. Lucy picks her up, strokes her and the cat kneads her and purrs loud as a motor. As I pass behind them on my way to the kitchen, I glance down.

Dear Robert,

I believe I saw you at the cinema last night, watching *La*

Grande Illusion. Perhaps now you will know how to dig your escape tunnel…

She is writing a letter to Desnos and at once I am back in Adrienne Monnier's shop in 1929, listening to Robert read his poems, entranced. There is Lucy, fluttering like a butterfly and Adrienne, grave and matriarchal in her long grey skirt, listening and advising.

André, who was never a favourite of Adrienne's, has told us that the German photographer who ousted Sylvia Beach in Adrienne's affections before the war, has left, that Adrienne and Sylvia are living together again, 'but as nuns, not as Sapphics'. At this distance, it is difficult to separate gossip from fact. Stories tangle, collide, spin off, metamorphose into mere fantasy, lines of desire scribbled at an oak table by the light of a yellow lamp.

We eat in silence – or, rather, I eat in silence – while she sips a glass from the bottle that Adèle has left. It is all Adèle's fault, I think, knowing that this is irrational and unfair. Her belief that food and wine bring pleasure leavens her otherwise severe personality. I leave a quarter of a sweet omelette on a plate and Lucy tastes it, eats two mouthfuls then pushes it away.

'Try a little more, dear heart.' I hate sounding like the mother of a stubborn three-year-old (at times like this, I think of Gabriella).

Lucy eats three more mouthfuls. I feel victorious. I feel exhausted. The doctor speaks of physiology, of imbalances of sodium and potassium. He uses words, 'oedema' and 'electrolytes', which are beautiful and strange but hold little meaning. He only tries to treat the scarred organs which cause her bloating and breathlessness; doesn't see the other damage.

I take up the plate and feed the rest to Chou-chou.

For dessert, there are pomegranates, and the sight of the fruit with its bursting scarlet sacs momentarily revives her. She takes one up, holds it in an outstretched hand as tenderly as you would hold a skull and intone, '*As soon as you eat of this fruit, your eyes will be opened and you will be LIKE GODS, knowing good from evil…* Demand the flavourful fruit. There is ONLY ONE. Ask for it without delay! You have nothing to lose.'

I take up the flavourful fruit and hold it aloft as I dance slowly around the table, chanting, '*Serpents in luminous rings form supple letters…*' but I see that she has lost interest in Eve's story which she wrote so long ago.

She sits down at the oak table and continues her letter to Desnos. I read *Melange* by Valéry, another of the recently dead. Occasionally, I look up and catch her eye; the night wears on until she puts down her pen.

'Come to bed.'

The wind has risen. We hear the sea's distant roil. Tomorrow it will rain, confining us to the house. She rolls over until her full length is against me, tells me that, despite everything, she wants to live. We kiss, slowly. I hear the mad pounding of her heart as she mounts me.

'Stop. This is dangerous for you.'

'Life is dangerous,' she replies, as she moves rhythmically against me then thrusts her fingers inside, using them until I cry out.

I tell her I want to give her the same pleasure but she says, no, enough, it's enough that I see your own. She draws the sheet over her swollen legs, which are always hidden in trousers or long skirts now. I know she hates what illness has done to her body; I know she is proud and does not want it discussed. We lie side by side and wonder what has become of Otto, who we have not heard from since the day the prison gates were opened. If he made it back, he has vanished into a Germany busy with reconstruction and amnesia.

I turn off the lamp, draw the coverlet around her. Tonight, she sleeps soundly but mine is fitful, fragmented by the watch I always keep.

She is gone when I wake, just as the night fades. I lie for a few moments, disorientated, my jagged sleep tugging me back to oblivion; then I get up and walk through the house, calling her. Sweat ridges my spine. In every room I enter, I expect to find her collapsed, prostrate, but there is only Chou-chou, who follows me, loudly demanding to be fed. I give the cat scraps of cold chicken then I lift my eyes to the window which overlooks the cemetery, where we once saw the Germans burying their dead.

She's there, of course. She has climbed over the wall, descended into death, moves among the rows of headstones, white as clamouring teeth. She is still dressed in her nightgown, is wearing one dark glove, one white, and carries something in one hand. She stops. She stands among the lilies which border one side of the graves and attaches the mask.

Her face a white ovoid; bland moon, barren and featureless. It hides a stretching sickness which took hold when she heard of Desnos's death from typhus in Teresienstadt; he survived the camp, could not survive its liberation. (Henri has written to us, told us that as Desnos's remains were transported through the streets of Paris towards their burial site, people came out of the cafés and fell to their knees on the street.)

We have seen the photographs of Belsen, images of genocide and extermination.

What happens to someone when her world becomes knowable only as an abattoir turned charnel house?

My hands shake as I take up the camera. It's cold outside. There's wet grass outside the cemetery gate which clings to my skirt, drenching the hem.

'Lucy, Lucy.' I speak to her how a stable hand might soothe a frightened horse.

She takes off the mask. Her eyes are glazed, fixed on her private horror.

Click.

She replaces the mask.

Click. Click.

The sound is immense in this walled seclusion. She stands amid the lilies, a zombie Madonna, eyeless and soulless.

When the roll of film is finished, I put her camera in the pocket of my skirt and join her in the flowers.

'You cannot mourn forever. Robert is not coming back. He would want you to go on.'

The words sound banal as I utter them, like something she would make fun of, capitalise and italicise, if she were to ever write them down: What makes you think he's COMING BACK? Do you think your ideas are SO IMPORTANT? *There are no guarantees* and HEAVEN has been DEFERRED!

Nevertheless, I proffer them, like a sleazy priest enticing a pilgrim with a relic.

For a moment, she makes no reply. There is only the sound of her overreaching heart, banging like a captive on the bars of its cage, then slowly, eyes fixed on some transparent world ahead, she recites the opening lines from Desnos's poem 'Epitaph':

> I lived in those times. For a thousand years
> I have been dead. Not fallen but hunted…

I catch her as she falls against me and we stumble towards the house.

finale

December 1954

Today, I covered all the mirrors in the house. If I knew the words, I, the goy, the shiksa, would say the Mourner's Kaddish; as it is I take the camera and walk once more to the beach.

A lowering sky. Snow drifts, glacial confetti on a wind which numbs my face. I am married to emptiness. Language recedes in a smooth grey tide. This is what happens, at the moment when the 'we' becomes an 'I'. Now, there are no words, just a snow-covered mound facing the sea and myself, this woman.

Shall I walk into the waves? No. I, who have always been the strong one, have not the courage to die. Not yet. There may come a time for that. For now, I am the enduring one, the ghost who continues.

Towards the end, the doctor was kind; he has always been kind. I think he knew what she and I were to each other. When I approached him last year about a possible journey to Paris, he said, 'Of course, certainly, take your friend. It won't make any difference now.'

As I left the surgery and walked towards St Brelade's Bay, the water azure beneath the summer sun, I saw him gazing down at me from the window with sadness and, I think, some pity. I flinched, as though his gaze was a barb, but later, when Lucy lay in the thin hospice bed, there was no pity, only courtesy and concern. 'Please let this lady be with her friend whenever she wants,' I overheard him tell the nurse in charge and that was why I was able to see Lucy's spirit go down the long white corridor at three a.m. I was holding her in my arms and I saw it move through the door to somewhere else. No pain; quietly. She made no sound, uttered no word of farewell: she was beyond that by then.

Yesterday, there were simple rites in the Fisherman's Chapel, the coffin lying before the rough stone altar. Breton, incapacitated by influenza, was not there, so in the end it was me, Adèle and Michaux: inconsolable. The self-aggrandising brother could not be reached – although I didn't try very hard – so we were at least spared his presence.

The wind throws gritty flurries of sand against my ankles. The water heaves and throws up gusts of spray when it hits the shore. Up ahead, I see the wife of one of the local pharmacists, someone with whom we had a passing acquaintance over the years. A handsome red-headed woman, this acquaintance, rather vain about her svelte figure, which she likes to display in tightly-belted coats and clinging blouses, and someone I know will want to extend conventional sympathy. What am I to say to her? Oh, yes, thank you, it was a very peaceful end, she looked as beautiful as a wax doll lying beneath the sheet and yes, this morning, as I passed along the corridor from bedroom to kitchen, I caught a glimpse of her face in the hand-beaten Mexican mirror given to her by Max Ernst and I stepped back, hoping to see her again…

No, I will say nothing at all to this good woman who I know worships every Sunday at St Mary and St Peter. So I leave the beach, turn so quickly I catch my heel and almost fall, scurry up the sand until I reach the concrete barricade of the sea wall which Lucy and I watched being built by the slaves. Keep going, keep going: I force my ageing body along. My breath wheezes, my knees ache.

I reach the road. Since I left the house, I have walked much further than I intended. St Aubin's Bay stretches in a steely arc before me. I take the camera from my coat pocket and frame the solitary figure on the beach, tiny against the great sky, the foreground bisected by the implacable wall.

I press the shutter. I make my final portrait: the lone woman walking on the beach, the stranger in the world.

I turn back towards the empty house waiting for me. I think about walking back to the water's edge, to where the icy frill of foam embellishes the sand, and casting the camera far out to sea. Let it sink, a piece of mechanical flotsam, a dysfunctional Cyclops, to the bottom, to be whirled about by tides and carried to the tropics where seahorses sing.

No: earth is always earth. I, the practical one, will refrain from all histrionic gestures. I will give it to André. He can add it to his vast collection, one more item for his shed of treasures: faded and torn antique maps, imitation suits of armour, chess sets with a missing pawn.

But I am being unkind to characterise his collecting as a mere mania for junk: the wheelchair he provided when we finally reached Paris worked perfectly. I pushed Lucy along the streets in the sixth arrondisement, feeling like a tourist in my own history. There was the Café de Flore, there was Les Deux Magots, where we caught a glimpse of Sartre and de Beauvoir, the new idols, as we passed. Sartre, the little man with the wall eye in love with Lenin has condemned surrealism as naive; this in turn had elicited predictable rage and contempt from André, so Lucy and I finally came to rest in an unfamiliar café near a church and a fountain, a place we had never visited.

There was André, effusive, waving over the waiter, full of talk about his new love, anarchism and dismissing 'that Stalinist, Sartre. Existentialism is just a passing craze based on post-war exhaustion', he told us. 'It means nothing.'

Max Ernst was there, nodding in agreement, and a newcomer, the squat uncongenial Czech, Toyen. I could see Lucy struggling to maintain interest, interjecting eagerly, too eagerly, while I, dutiful nursemaid, sipped a café crème and ate pastry. I watched Toyen eye Lucy's skirt and blouse, trying to estimate the cost like any bourgeois housewife; she wasn't to know that beneath the stylish new clothes there was a spider body, spindly legs jutting from a bloated abdomen. I poured Lucy water, listened to an argument which had broken out between Breton and Ernst, some sort of tired circular thing which made the whole occasion feel as though we were actors in a second-rate farce.

We left soon after, promising to return the following week, and I pushed the chair away, taking care the wheels didn't catch between stones. We did go back, once more, then took the train to St Malo without regret.

Spitting coldness of spray on my face forces me back to the present. The tide is running full and waves hurl themselves against the barrier. In a nearby field, a group of horses stand with their heads bowed, rumps flagellated by the wind. Always when I return to the present, it is with the sick knowledge that she is gone; that I suffer from a malaise which will not end.

What if this burden becomes too great to bear? Then I will put it down. She lived courageously and died courageously; let it be so for me.

I press on towards St Brelade's Bay, taking the main road because in this weather the back lanes are muddy and dangerous; a fall could injure me and leave me alone for hours, even days, while I waited for a passerby. A gust of wind so strong almost lifts me off my feet. Palm tree fronds swirl, dervish-mad.

Bitter pellets of hail spear my cheeks as I pass the St Brelade's Bay hotel, now taking visitors again, with a recently installed swimming pool in which German tourists swim. Despite the wind and the ground glazed with ice, I pause; I know I must enter the empty house, hear my footsteps on the grey kitchen flagstones and face the mirrors, black as dead suns. Chou-chou will be there, wanting food. I raise my eyes to the windows, glimpse a jagged grey shape pierced with red and cry out, thinking it's a wandering ghost, heart aflame, returned.

But then I see it's mere reflection, Adèle in a grey raincoat with red jacket beneath, holding the child Raphael by the hand as they come towards me. The boy is inadequately dressed, in grey jumper and dark pants. This is probably not caused by his grandmère's lack of care but because he is a stubborn little thing, constantly fighting her authority. In this way, in his obstinate independence, he is like Adèle, like his mother too; and who could have predicted that accident at the Normandy crossroads two years ago, Gabriella's car concertinaed by the truck's impact. (Others also gone, including the Baron, his funeral well-attended by the island's great and good.)

But now this child has become the light of Adèle's life, the sentimental phrase failing to diminish the enamoured gaze she bends on him. His yellow-white curls have not darkened with age; these, and something quick and sharp in his movements, remind me occasionally of Otto. (There is a possible reason for this, of course, but it is too preposterous to entertain seriously.)

The boy sees me and waves. I raise my hand, wave back, and in that moment know that I cannot live in a mausoleum. I will sell the house, keep some books and photos, display the medal Lucy was awarded in 1951 for our wartime activities. (Me a shadow as usual, unrecognised; doesn't matter, I have her medal.)

It waits for me now, this silent unlit building, but before I begin to ascend the steps leading to the gate, knowing that I will soon have to move, to speak, to act in the postscript of my life, I turn my gaze to the sea, think about the cold fathoms of churning water. In the distance, westward, I see the concrete gun tower, eunuch sentinel. The wind is dying as evening the approaches. An anaemic sun pokes briefly through dark blotting clouds; by morning, the ocean will be pane-flat. Another day.

I see Adèle smile and call but her words don't reach me. I remember the first day we met at Café Gitane, when Lucy dangled from the trellis, caught in a lattice of light and shade as I pressed the shutter. The image fixed at that moment of history, a figure swinging on the cusp of hope and destruction.

I place my foot on the first step. With the other, I push off. The stone flight looms ahead.

What is the point of saying, 'I love you'? I only wish to be able to think it very forcefully, near you, in the silence.

Author's Note

Suzanne Malherbe remained on Jersey until 1972 when, aged eighty and in declining health, she ended her life with an overdose of barbiturates. She and Lucy are buried together on Jersey. Their tombstone bears a Star of David and words by William Blake: *I saw a new Heaven and a new Earth.*

Interest has grown in the lives and work of Lucy Schwob and Suzanne Malherbe since the mid-1980s. In 2018, their Resistance activities were recognised when a Paris street was named after them. In 2020, a series of eight commemorative stamps featuring their artwork was launched on Jersey.

This story collection is based on actual events; however, it is a work of fiction and, apart from those characters clearly recognisable in history, no one depicted in the collection bears any relation to any human being, living or dead.

My research for the story collection was drawn from diverse sources but *Don't kiss me: the art of Claude Cahun and Marcel Moore,* edited by Louise Downie, has been particularly helpful. The quoted passages Claude Cahun's monograph 'Heroines' which appear on pages 12, 43, 63, 66, 71, 92 and 93 are taken from *Inverted Odysseys: Claude Cahun, Maya Deren, Cindy Sherman,* edited by Shelley Rice. Other quoted passages, on pages 25, 27, 51, 77 and 101, are taken from Claude Cahun's *Aveux nos avenus,* published in English as *Disavowed Confessions.*

The song Suzanne sings to Lucy on page 13 is an extract from the medieval troubadour ballad 'Foy Porter' by Guillaume de Machant.

The incident depicted on page 94 concerning the passage of Robert Desnos's body through Paris is taken from the second volume of Simone de Beauvoir's memoirs, *The Prime of Life.*

The images on pages 6, 38, 48, 52, 62, 78 and 86 are the collaboration of Claude Cahun and Marcel Moore, those on pages 20 and 96 by Marcel Moore.

www.ingramcontent.com/pod-product-compliance
Lightning Source LLC
Chambersburg PA
CBHW030820200726
48288CB00004B/1317